Also by Delacorta

DIVA
NANA
LUNA

LOLA

A NOVEL

BY DELACORTA

Translated by Victoria Reiter

SUMMIT BOOKS
NEW YORK

This novel is a work of fiction. Names, characters, places and incidents are either the product of the author's imagination or are used fictitiously. Any resemblance to actual events or locales or persons, living or dead, is entirely coincidental.

Published by SUMMIT BOOKS
A Division of Simon & Schuster,
Inc.
Simon & Schuster Building
1230 Avenue of the Americas
New York, New York 10020

Originally published in French under the title *Rock*
Designed by Daniel Chiel
Manufactured in the United States of America

1 3 5 7 9 10 8 6 4 2

Library of Congress Cataloging in Publication Data

Odier, Daniel, 1945–
Lola.

Translation of: Rock.
I. Title.
PZ2675.D5R613 1984 843'.914 84-8758
ISBN 0-671-47752-8

For Jacques and Anne

CHAPTER

1

IT WAS NOVEMBER, THE MONTH of dark skies, rain and death.

Serge Gorodish had spent the last week sitting at his Steinway, practicing two- and three-part *Inventions* by Johann Sebastian Bach. Not only did the music fill his soul with rapture, it also put him in a mood conducive to the creation and development of new ideas. A premonitory shiver ran through him: Gorodish was on the brink of discovery.

Alba was so keenly aware of his state of mind that she kept out of his way, using the free afternoons to transform herself. She was bored with loud colors and gaudy clothes, tired of glitter and flash. As she grew more womanly she found herself wanting to resemble American actresses of the fifties, the women who had starred in *films noirs,* crime melodramas. She had already spent five thousand francs on new clothes: the sultry result was enough to make a Goldwyn or a Warner Brother gasp.

The tempo slowed, Bach turned into Webern. Gorodish's fingers hovered over the keyboard. Suddenly he clapped his hands to his forehead and gave a war whoop. The Steinway's strings vibrated in harmony. He sat absolutely still for a moment, pictures flashing through his mind like fifty movies projected simultaneously on a single screen. Holding back a heartfelt "Eureka!" he rose from the piano and settled himself in his favorite easy chair. Leaning back, he closed his eyes and felt phantom bank notes raining down, covering him like leaves falling from a money tree.

Alba stepped out of the elevator. Surprised not to hear the piano, she let her pile of packages slip to the floor.

Gorodish opened his eyes and saw an unfamiliar Alba standing over him. Her adolescent body appeared to have been poured into a tight tube of black jersey. Her adorable face smiled down at him from beneath the wisp of black veil that floated from the brim of her hat. Alba's long blond hair, gathered in a braid, lay draped over her left shoulder. The tight sleeves of the dress revealed a thin band of gleaming wrist. Her hands were hidden in fine black gloves. Sheer black stockings and high-heeled alligator pumps completed the outfit.

"*The Big Sleep,*" Alba announced in a voluptuous voice.

"You're sublime! Come kiss me, my Queen of the Night!"

"You'll faint when you hear what it cost."

"I can tell that dress didn't come from a secondhand store. Why don't you go back and buy yourself another one in flannel?"

"I thought we were almost broke."

"Ever since we met I've been trying to come up with an idea for a deal, a *brilliant* idea for a deal, and I think I've found it. Before we're through we're going to need a bulldozer to scoop up the money!"

Alba moved toward him, her hips weaving. For a moment Gorodish felt like Howard Hawks. Something in his mind

shouted “Action!” and the camera moved in for a close-up.
Alba delicately lifted the veil. A short, hard jab and Bogart hit the floor, Gorodish taking his place just in time to taste the subtle perfume of her slightly parted lips.

CHAPTER

2

ALBA SLID ONTO GORODISH'S lap, caressed his forehead, kissed him lightly and said, "What's your new idea?"

"Like most great ideas, this one is fairly simple. It occurred to me that there are any number of people out there who know something we could use, but they have no outlet for their information so they simply keep it to themselves. Just think of it: all those ideas, just sitting there, waiting for us! I've been trying to figure out a way to siphon off some of that information and I think I've hit on the perfect scheme. We're going to set up an information brokerage service. We'll use whatever money we have left to finance an advertising campaign, then sit back and wait. I guarantee you we'll be swamped with calls."

"What kind of an ad campaign?" Alba asked, her eyebrows quivering with interest.

"I thought we'd place a full-page ad in *France-Soir, Le Figaro* and *Le Monde,* all the daily papers. A one-line ad saying,

"Something you know might be worth a lot of money . . ." with the name of our company and our telephone number at the bottom of the page."

"We'll get a lot of crank calls."

"Of course we will, but we'll also get a lot of information worth its weight in gold. You know people are always looking for a way to make some easy money."

"It's a wonderful idea."

"And the best thing about it is we'll be operating within the law. At least in principle."

"That's no fun."

"You won't be bored, I promise. This is no one-shot deal. A project like this could go on forever. Now, the first thing we must do is think up a name for the company. Then we have to buy the advertising space. . . ."

"Let's call it Alba-Info International."

"Very good. And we'll set up an office. . . ."

"I'll be your secretary, at least at the beginning. It'll be fun and we'll have a chance to get organized before we bring in an outsider."

Alba rose and paraded up and down before Gorodish, displaying herself like a fashion model on a runway. She planted herself in front of him and, with an enigmatic smile on her lips, said, "Carpaccio."

"You've suddenly developed an interest in Italian Renaissance painters."

"I'm talking about food," Alba said. "It's a Venetian recipe. Very thin layers of rump steak pounded flat, with olive oil and lemon juice trickled over it. And a bottle of Frascati. How does that sound?"

"So good that I'm drooling. Do I have time to practice my *Inventions* while you're making dinner?"

"Yes. Can we buy a tape recorder?"

"I don't see why not," Gorodish said, his fingers reaching for the still-warm piano keys.

CHAPTER

3

As a result of the first advertisement in *Le Figaro,* the morning paper, they received a dozen calls and made appointments to meet with several of the callers. However, when the ad appeared in *France-Soir,* the major evening paper, the telephone began to ring off the hook.

Alba and Gorodish screened the callers by the simple expedient of asking them what they had for sale. An amazingly large percentage obliged by divulging at least part of their information.

The telephone rang again.

"Alba-Info International," Alba said sweetly.

"Uh, hello," a man said hesitantly, "is this Alba-Info International?"

"Yes, sir. May I help you?"

"I, uh, want to talk to the head of the company."

"One moment, please, I'll see if he's available."

Alba nodded at Gorodish. He picked up the receiver.

"Is this the, uh, president?"

"Yes. You have something of interest that you wish to sell?"

"Maybe. But I'm not going to tell you anything yet. I want to know something before I . . ."

"What did you wish to know?"

"Uh, well, how much, I mean, how much do you pay?" the man asked nervously.

For some reason Gorodish sensed that he had hooked a live one. "It all depends on what you have to sell. We usually manage to work out a mutually satisfying . . ."

"This is worth a lot of money."

"I'm sure it is," Gorodish said soothingly, "and I'm willing to pay exactly what it's worth. . . ."

"I'll have to think it over. Listen, you're not dealing with some dummy here. You're going to have to fork over. . . ."

"Why don't you come see me?" Gorodish suggested. "We'll talk it over."

"I don't know. There's something funny about your ad."

"You called us," Gorodish said dryly. "Nobody twisted your arm."

"Oh, don't pretend you're insulted. I'm sitting on a gold mine here and if you want a piece of my action you're going to have to pay through the nose. . . ."

Alba was listening in on the extension.

"I can only repeat my invitation: come see me. If you're not satisfied with the fee we offer you can always take your information elsewhere, sell it to someone . . ."

"Yeah, I've heard that one before. You're really curious now, aren't you? I know you've got some real money behind you: anybody who spends that much on an ad has to have a few, right? But I got a hunch there's something not quite kosher about your agency. I'm going to have to watch my step with you."

"I can only repeat: it all depends on what you have to sell."

"How about if I said my brother went to Canada when he was twenty-three? What would you pay for that?"

"What's your brother doing in Canada?"

"Pretty fast on your feet, aren't you? He works in a fish cannery. I don't even know why I gave you that much. Let's get back to business: this thing I want to sell is the goods, but I need to take a look at you, see if I can trust you before I deal. After all, I don't know you from Adam, do I?"

"I've asked you to come here. . . ."

"Oh, no, you don't. I know all those tricks; I've seen those movies. You probably got cameras and microphones hidden all over the place. You get me over there and drug me or pressure me to tell . . . you're probably trying to trace this call right now, aren't you? Well, it won't do you any good: I'm calling from a phone booth."

"You suggest something, then."

"You know Place Pereire? There's a café there, the Royal-Pereire. You be there tonight at eight. Sit in the front window and order two crème de menthes. I'll look you over and decide if I can trust you or not."

"Until tonight, then," Gorodish said, hanging up. "A flake."

"We ought to do something to relax," Alba said.

"Knowing you, you have something specific in mind."

"Naturally. I want you to take me to the Folies Bergère, or the Moulin-Rouge, someplace like that."

"You think they'll let you in?" Gorodish asked, amused.

"Of course," Alba replied, lowering the veil over her eyes and pulling a long silver cigarette holder from her purse.

CHAPTER 4

GORODISH SAT IN THE ROYAL-Pereire, sipping a glass of Bordeaux, two ponies of green crème de menthe standing on the table before him.

"Telephone call for Madame Alba Info," the hostess brayed.

Gorodish jumped up and headed for the telephone booth. "I've been waiting over half an hour," he said irritably. "I expect the people with whom I do business to be on time."

"Take it easy; I was here before you. I watched you come in and I've been looking you over, trying to make up my mind. You can't blame me for being careful, can you?"

"All right, but let's get on with it. Make up your mind right now or I'm leaving."

"You don't look anything like what I expected. I think maybe we can do some business."

"I haven't said I'm interested, yet," Gorodish replied in a bland voice.

"Yeah? Well, this is something special." The man seemed

more confident now. "I hope you've got a heavy line and some really solid hooks. You an angler?"

"No."

"Too bad. You look the pike type to me."

"Oh? And what type are you?"

"I'm much more common, much easier to hook. I'm stout-backed, bullheaded and voracious. I've got a big mouth, with barbels on each side of it. I'm a freshwater fish," the voice said warningly. "I live in deep ponds, lakes, slow-moving rivers, in backwaters. I live in the deepest, murkiest channels. I'm a bottom feeder: I love that thick bottom growth. I feed heaviest on rainy days, like today. In fact, I've really worked up an appetite."

"You're a catfish," Gorodish said, amused.

"I thought you didn't know anything about angling."

"There's angling, and then there's angling. You shouldn't believe everything people tell you."

"Let's get down to business. You have the money?"

"Show me the bait."

"I want five big ones for this."

"Let's just say it's a definite maybe."

"You see? I knew we could do business."

"You're greedy."

"That's how it is with catfish. We roam the bottom, scooping up everything that comes our way."

"I thought catfish could be scupped with worms."

"Paper's better. Especially paper with the picture of a president on it."

"When do you want to meet?"

"I'm in no hurry."

"Whatever suits," Gorodish said, shrugging, "but you're going to have to give me a taste. What's this all about?"

"You like rock music? Hard rock?"

"Not especially."

"Well, it doesn't really matter. You ever heard of Lola Black?"

"The name sounds vaguely familiar."

"Good. Check into it, see if it's worth anything to you. I'll call again."

Outside was the night, the rain, the light reflected on the asphalt pavement: perfect weather for a catfish.

CHAPTER

5

GORODISH HAD SPENT PART OF the afternoon at Lido-Musique. Now, leaving his umbrella in the entry hall, he walked into the living room to find Alba seated on the carpet, blow-drying her long blond hair. She was looking especially beautiful in a midnight blue peignoir. Alba shut off the hair dryer and kissed Gorodish.

"You bought a new album."

"Go sit in the easy chair and I'll play it for you."

He put *Fires*, Lola Black's last album, on the turntable. A torrent of heavy metal rock poured from the speakers. Alba burst out laughing. "Serge, you're crazy!" she shouted.

Gorodish listened for a moment and then lowered the sound. "You recognize her?"

"Of course: that's the Lola Black Band. She used to be the number one heavy metal rock star. She was a genius."

"*Was?*"

"Don't you know anything? She killed herself or drowned

or something. They found her body washed up on a beach in California."

"Are you sure?"

"There were headlines and stories all over the papers; it was big news, just as big as if Haydn or Beethoven had done himself in." Alba laughed. "Did you ever meet that man who called?"

"No."

"Why this sudden interest in Lola Black?"

"Catfish mentioned her."

"What?"

"The man who called: he thinks he's a catfish. He telephoned me at the Royal-Pereire and said that he has important information about Lola Black. He insisted I do some research on the subject before his next call. That's why I bought the album."

"There's a movie about her playing at Videostone, on Rue des Grands-Augustins. That's not too far from here: why don't we go see it?"

"Good idea. I have a feeling he'll be calling again tomorrow."

The film, a compilation of several documentaries made while Lola Black was still alive, opened with a flash of red and blue strobe lights and the sound of the band working itself into a frenzy over the introduction to her first number. The music was lyrical and violent. Reflecting that life was forever filled with surprises, Gorodish sat back and watched the movie. The screen went black as the band counted out several long bars filled with a pounding, sizzling silence. Then the crowd began to whistle and shout and white spotlights punched a path between two HiWatt speakers as the lead guitar laid down a hot, ascending line. And the rock star appeared in all her splendor, her body nervy and long-muscled, her movements feline and electric as she strode up and down the incandescent stage. There was an undercurrent of hesitation, of contained passion, in her gestures. She stared out at the audience, probing it, gauging its mood. Hysterical cries. Bodyguards grabbed a boy as he tried to jump up onstage.

Lola simply stood there and she owned the place. Her arm rose, etching a slow arc in the air. The mike in her other hand moved toward her lips and suddenly it began: a shriek of sound.

Tommy Bonaparte, on percussion, wore a bishop's miter on his head. Sitting Bull Plastic, on lead guitar, wore buckskin pants, the peace pipe thrust through his belt bobbing and dangling as he hopped up and down. He toked on it all through the set, taking a hit or two, or three, each time. Mexico Flat, on bass guitar, wore jeans underneath a filthy bridal gown. His body was long and emaciated. His greasy black hair, cut in a modified Mohawk, waved wildly from the crown of his head.

Lola's long dark hair whipped around her face as her body contorted and gathered in on itself. She stood almost immobile, the musicians moving around her like satellites gravitating around a planet. She kissed each of them, and the crowd screamed. Out of that scream came the first bars of "Fire," twenty-two minutes of heavy metal designed to make the sun go nova.

A string on Mexico Flat's bass snapped. He roared and smashed the instrument to the floor, jumping on it with both feet and howling, his howls melding into licks from the drums, the guitar and Lola's throat. A long-haired acolyte came onstage carrying a new bass. Mexico Flat grabbed it, stroked it, and the heat coming from the group went up a notch.

Lola stood still. The music faded until it was no more than a sigh, a presence felt rather than heard. She chanted a long, tremulous poem, her body trembling with intensity, the camera moving in close on her vibrant face to reveal eyes filled with liquid cocaine tears. The audience went berserk. Lola, high priestess of rock, drank in the applause, the adulation carrying her even higher until she was floating above the delirium. And the beat began again, steel and blood, scalding and surging and goading her on.

The music turned Gorodish inside out. He rode its rhythms, feeling them seething through his body like a subterranean river of lava. His arm went around Alba's shoulders and she pressed against him, taking advantage of the lull caused by the first interview to kiss him. It was rare that Alba could not find a beat or two of dead time in a movie, moments long enough for her to grope Gorodish and murmur words of passion.

Sitting Bull Plastic sat in a recording studio, precariously perched on a stool. The camera watched as he slopped up coffee from a white Styrofoam cup. The interviewer, Phil Mann, said:

"You've been with Lola from the very beginning. What does her death mean to you?"

Sitting Bull Plastic lifted tired, disdainful eyes toward the interviewer, took one last swallow of coffee, put the cup down on a speaker and mumbled into the microphone:

"You know, like, Lola, her dyin' an' all that, it's like she really fucked that big nothingness out there, beat those goddamn bastards, all them toothbrush manufacturers, you know, that buncha assholes always sayin' things like 'I got me a pedigree Lhasa apso belonged to Bob Dylan's uncle' . . . you know . . . shee-it, she fucked the big nothingness, an' that's all she wrote."

Sitting Bull Plastic rose and kicked the speaker, knocking over the Styrofoam cup. The camera pulled back to follow him out of the studio, the interviewer trotting behind him, mike in one outstretched hand.

More music.

Guzzy Smith, Lola's manager, sitting in the backseat of his Rolls, wearing an Apache war bonnet and a white suit:

"Far as I was concerned Lola was 'The Divine.' They used to call Garbo 'The Divine,' and they call Bette Midler 'The

Divine,' but compared to Lola, they just don't cut it. Three albums, certified platinum; they even wanted me to book her some gigs on Mars and Venus; you go ask them guys floating around in *Sputnik* or *Voyager,* or whatever."

A VOICE-OVER: "Can you tell us what really happened: the true story behind her disappearance and death?"

"It's all on account of them silent majority, born-again evangelicals and all them walking dead. I got NASA to investigate it, too, same's I did, only they used different methods, scientifically guaran-damn-teed."

"What happened?"

"We were booked for a concert at Family Dog in San Francisco. Lola was really cooking: even the ocean went real quiet when she began to sing. We'd set up a tour for after, but at the end of that concert all them silent, born-again evangelicals turned their lights on Lola. She'd sung her guts out but they gave her a breakdown, no lie. Instant insanity. She called off the tour, said she had to go find The Great Spirit of the Forest, he was s'posed to be waiting for her down at Big Sur where she had this cabin. Anyway, I drove Lola down there. She wanted to be alone so I left. I came back a week later, just to check, you know; the cabin was empty. I thought maybe she'd gone out to meditate in the woods, you know, gone out there looking for that mystical union with The Great Spirit. You gotta respect that. So I waited. For two days. They sent out a search party, but she'd disappeared. Her body turned up on the beach, I guess it musta been a month later, and I had to go down to identify her. Her head'd been cut off: you could hardly tell it was her."

"Was it murder, or suicide?"

"Fuck off," Guzzy Smith said, motioning to his chauffeur to drive on.

Several other pieces of film followed, including a clip from the program on which Lola had first appeared on nationwide television. Her early style had been polite and well-bred, yet she had already shown signs of a singular intensity.

The film ended with part of the Family Dog concert during which the *Fires* album had been recorded live: absolutely space drive.

The last shot was a medium close-up of an exhausted Lola as she lay on the stage. In the background the band was smashing everything in sight. Then they, too, were reduced to silence. The camera moved in closer on Lola's face as she sprawled, unconscious, on the stage. The cameraman got a guitar in the gut for his trouble, the camera swinging wildly, unfocused, arching up and then down again as he fell.

Gorodish and Alba left the theater. It was raining. Holding hands, they strolled along the quays of the Seine.

"We'll buy her other albums tomorrow," Gorodish said.

CHAPTER 6

THE PEOPLE AT *ROCK AND FOLK* magazine were friendly but, unfortunately, Phil Mann hadn't come in yet. Alba pulled out all the stops and managed to wheedle his home address out of them.

The address turned out to be that of a broken-down hotel that looked as if its moment of splendor had ended a century earlier. The concierge, who resembled an undertaker, directed her to room number seventeen on the second floor.

Alba knocked at the door. "Come in," a man's voice shouted.

Phil Mann was seated at a desk, sipping a stinger and pounding on a pre–World War II Underwood portable typewriter. Alba immediately recognized him as the interviewer in the film she and Gorodish had seen the night before. He was tall and thin and was wearing jeans that looked as if they had been tapered by an amateur seamstress. He rubbed his forehead, pushing back long black locks to reveal electric eyes and an angel-dust mouth.

"Hi. My name's Alba."

"You look like an Alba," Phil said. "Hold on a minute, I just have to finish this article." Without pausing to think he typed: "An angel just walked in. To be continued (if I survive). Ciao."

"It's a quarter column short," he said, "but they'll fill in with a photo or something."

Records and magazines lay stacked in uneasy equilibrium on one corner of his desk. Before Alba could protest Phil took a Polaroid camera from atop the pile and snapped her picture.

She edged forward to watch it develop. Phil pinned the photograph to his wall, saying: "Not bad for the first time. How about the two of us getting together for an instant replay? We'll do our own version of *The Bad and the Beautiful.*"

"Not now," Alba said, "I need my after-school snack."

"Gotcha." Phil picked up the telephone. It took several long seconds before someone answered. Alba inspected the pictures of rock and movie stars pinned to all four walls of the room, his clothing strewn on the floor, the large poster of Marilyn Monroe in the nude. Speakers dangled from the ceiling, their wires leading to a drawer under the bed. Alba peered beneath it and saw a small stereo set.

"Hey, bring us something to eat . . . anything you've got . . . all right: I'll mention you in my next column."

"I like what you write," Alba said.

"Yeah; me, too: especially this last one I just finished. Where do you read my stuff?"

"In *Rock, La Libération, les Nouvelles littéraires.* You've written several articles about Lola Black. . . ."

"Yeah. There's this one thing I did that was really special." He pawed through a pile of brightly colored file folders. "Actually, I did two big articles about her. The first one was a kind of psychological profile. Or, you could call it a rap sheet, if you're into cops. Here, I'll read it to you." He seated himself on the unmade bed.

Lola Black Bio

Last Name: Nash
First Name: Virginia
Date of Birth: September 20, 1948
Place of Birth: Detroit, Michigan
Height: 5′6″
Weight: 115 lb
Blood Type O+

Tastes and Preferences
Favorite Food: French cheese
Favorite Drink: Burgundy
Smoke: Opium
Day: Every night of the week
Color: Two, in juxtaposition
Perfume: Sandalwood
Favorite city: New York
Second favorite city: Beaune
Animal: Man
Type of Entertainment: Silence
Metal: Heavy

Cultural Preferences
Writer: Arthur Rimbaud
Music: Music
Composers: From Monteverdi to Carla Bley
Singer: Lotte Lenya
Theater: Carmelo Bene
Movies: *Films noirs*
Actors: Edward G. Robinson, James Cagney
Actresses: Gene Tierney, Gloria Grahame
News: Daily
Philosopher: Lao-Tse
Historical personage: de Tocqueville
Historical event: The creation of the universe

Character and Personality Traits
Education: On the road
Religion: Pantheist

Best Trait: Acute sense of reality
Worst Trait: Acute sense of reality
Obsession: To communicate
Nervousness: Very
Violence: Onstage
Favorite place: Inside the body
Money: Lots
Best Memory: Being onstage
Worst Memory: Life
Enemy: The invisible crowd
Men: Alive
Hobby: Asshole question
Friendship: Is love

A fat bellman entered, winked at Phil and deposited a loaded tray on the bed. It held a pot of tea, two garlic-sausage sandwiches and four napoleon pastries.

"You've described her perfectly," Alba said.

"Don't you want your snack?"

"I'll eat later. Read me the other article."

LETTER TO NO ONE

Lola, this is Phil: remember? Albuquerque, June 1978. We met in a McDonald's. I'd written some articles about you. I was eating a hamburger. I looked at you. We smiled. Sitting Bull Plastic was with you and you asked me to join you.

I was a stranger. I could have been anybody. You might even have read some of my poems without knowing who wrote them. City Lights Books: that's more or less where my head was at. It was really good that night, Lola. I wrote a poem about your music, right there, at that pink Formica table. "Lola Night": remember? Sitting Bull stared out the window at the street bathed in light, fingering riffs in space.

You tilted your head to read the poem, then you read it again, and you looked at me with your big, soulful eyes. . . . I can still remember that moment . . . and you said:

"Phil."

We stood up and leaned over the table, over the plastic and the poem, and we kissed: space brother, space sister.

Sitting Bull said, "Alabama Uncle." He crawled over the back of the booth and walked out singing "Dark Deep Rock." Outside, some Chicano kids followed him, asking for his autograph and he panicked and began to run.

"He's really wild," you said.

We stayed there, just the two of us, smoking a joint until the McDonald's manager yelled at us in Spanish. When we left, the street was empty. All the kids had taken off after Sitting Bull.

We didn't have to say a word: the space between us was fluid and glittering with gold dust. We walked to where you'd parked your car, that old blue Ford that'd covered so much territory, the universe reflected in its corroded chrome, its seats gleaming under the streetlights. You turned on the radio. Billie Holiday was singing "My Man." I watched the moonlight gleaming in your tears.

When it was over you turned off the radio and said, real low, as if you were talking to heaven, "Billie."

We rode for hours. We didn't care where we were going. You parked the car deep in the desert, with that great milky light overhead, and you told me to kiss your hair. I kissed your hair and we looked at each other and took off our jeans. Your bikini panties were green. We made love while a Mexican crossing the desert on foot watched us, his eyes shining under the brim of his hat. Today, I echo you on that June night in Albuquerque.

I SAY LOLA
I SAY LOLA—THE WAY YOU SAID BILLIE
WITH THE SAME EMOTION
IN THE DESERT
I never saw you again but I loved you, just like all
the other men you'd had in that old Ford.
I loved you because you were Music.
The aching incarnation of Heavy Metal.
The cry that rouses the body.
The beauty of Rock wailing from your guts.
The heat of your eyes

And your voice saying: join us
and all that time you were wearing out
your discordant life,
Kicking it around in the Infinite
In the music of the silence when everything is smashed
and the amplifiers are hooked up to nothing.
And you fled, for you had just given up your life.
Like that night in June, when you said
to a perfect stranger, "Join us";
and Sitting Bull went running through the streets,
And you said Billie.
I say Lola.
There is no moon.
I am in a room, in New York
Sitting in front of my cold, heavy metal machine
And nothing illuminates my tears.

Alba was silent for a long moment. "Sonuvabitch," she said at last, "that's beautiful."

Phil leaned toward her, smiling soulfully. He had small, pointed teeth. "She touched me," he said, touching Alba.

CHAPTER 7

ALBA WANDERED AROUND THE neighborhood, unable to understand why she was feeling so guilty yet not daring to go home. She knew Gorodish would immediately sense her unease and would never believe she had backed off at the last minute. She began to wonder if she shouldn't have gone through with it after all, if only to drive Gorodish completely insane once and for all. Alba felt torn; her emotions seesawed back and forth. She did not really care whether she lost her virginity or not, whether she kept it like some relic of bygone days or gave it up. Her reaction had been purely physical: she simply did not want to make love with anyone but Gorodish.

Suddenly, an idea came to her: she would get thoroughly drunk before going back to the apartment. Gorodish would see nothing but that she was smashed, and she would bluff her way through it by telling him Phil Mann had given her something weird to drink. She had several of his magazine articles in her pocket to help back up her story.

Alba entered a bistro and ordered whiskey. The bartender handed her a soft drink. "Sorry, mademoiselle, but we've had inspectors hanging around here lately, have to be careful about serving minors."

"You pious old poop," Alba said icily. The bartender slid the glass of soda pop toward her.

Knowing that she would face the same problem everywhere she went, Alba did not even try going to another bar. Instead, she walked into the supermarket on the Rue de Buci and came out carrying a bottle of J&B Scotch. All she needed now was a quiet place to get sloshed. Not bothering to check what film was playing, Alba took refuge in a movie theater, settled herself in the back row and opened the bottle. The first swallow nearly stripped the flesh from her throat.

Alba left the theater, walked carefully to a nearby bench and eased herself onto it. She almost missed the seat.

In the dark of the theater she had felt quite normal, but here, in the light of day, it suddenly occurred to her that, just possibly, she had overdone it. Gotta get home, she thought. Gotta get home now, she thought, five or six times.

She tried to walk up Boulevard Saint-Germain but the dumb trees kept getting in her way.

It took awhile, but at last the taxi driver deciphered what she was trying to tell him. He helped her into the elevator and rode up with her.

Gorodish heard rumblings, mutterings and a man's voice. Alba was trying to keep her balance. Gorodish repressed a smile.

"Picked her up on Boulevard Saint-Germain," the driver said. "Looks like she's really tied one on."

Gorodish thanked him and paid the fare. Then he carried his angel into the bathroom, undressed her and held her under a cold shower, just to get her attention. Finally, he tucked her into bed.

"What happened?" he asked.

"You know, 'at guy a' *Rock and Folk*, Phil Mann, I was . . .

uh, we drank something, Suze, up at his place and he, uh . . ."

Gorodish pulled the curtains closed, saying, "Sleep now. You'll feel better later."

Alba's bed rolled and pitched on an ever-rising sea until, at last, she sank beneath the waves.

Gorodish could tell the difference between the aroma of Suze and the odor of whiskey. Alba was too smart to get drunk with someone she did not know, and Gorodish had noticed his nymph's hesitation and embarrassment as she tried to explain what had happened with Phil Mann. Gorodish thought he knew what had really happened.

He found a slip of paper with a telephone number jotted on it. "Good afternoon, madame. I was a client of yours six or seven months ago. . . ."

"May I have your name and address, please." The woman checked her files, then said, "Will there be something special this time? Any particular quirk . . ."

"Just a brunette, around thirty years old. . . ."

"Outcall, or here, in our comfortable facility?"

"Outcall, and as soon as possible."

"Lea will be there in half an hour. Will that be by the hour or will you want her to spend the night?"

"Two or three hours should do it."

Gorodish picked through his music scores until he found the Mozart *Fantasia* K.397. He played it straight through, five times.

Alba opened her eyes. Her head ached and her tongue felt as if it were pasted to her palate. She turned on the light and glanced at her watch. It was ten-thirty. She could hear Gorodish's voice, and a woman answering him.

She pinched herself, feeling the nails cutting into her skin and taking it as a sign that she was sober. Pulling on a pink-and-green-striped American T-shirt, she opened her bedroom door and headed for the living room.

The door to Gorodish's bedroom stood open. The bed was

unmade. A peach-colored suit, panties and a bra lay on the floor.

Alba walked into the living room. The woman was beautiful. She looked as if she had just stepped out of a magazine advertisement. There was a towel around her waist and she was just emptying the last of a bottle of champagne into a glass. Gorodish looked up at Alba. It seemed an eternity before he spoke: "Lea, this is Alba, my daughter."

Alba was ashen. She stood frozen in the doorway, tears pouring from her eyes, unable to shout the word "Bastard!" that was ringing in her head. Suddenly Alba turned and ran to her room, threw herself on the bed and wept, emptying herself of every last tear in her body.

"Maybe you ought to leave now, Lea," Gorodish said.

"You shouldn't have done that in front of your daughter. It shocked her so. Why don't we make it my place next time?"

"All right."

"Hello, this is Catfish."

"Oh," Gorodish said coldly.

"How'd you like the bait?"

"I looked into the matter, as you suggested, and frankly I don't think you have anything worth buying. Lola Black died six months ago in California. You ought to keep up with the news, read the papers, get yourself a subscription to *Rock and Folk*, it's a pretty good magazine. Or even read Phil Mann's column in *les Nouvelles littéraires.*"

"Hey, I'm not bullshitting you: I swear she's alive. I'm going to tell you something that'll shake you up: I've seen her. She's hiding out here in France, not far from this place I know."

"How could someone like you recognize a rock star? You aren't one of those closet music-video freaks, are you?"

"No. I've got a sixteen-year-old daughter who's crazy about rock. The house is full of Lola Black posters, so I recognized her the minute I saw her. It aroused my curiosity, so to speak. My daughter told me the girl was dead, but I went back there anyway, just to make sure. There's something fishy about where and how she's living. This could be a really good story. I bet there are a lot of people who'd like to know she's alive."

"Perhaps," Gorodish said. "I might just look into it."

"You bring me the cash and I'll give you the rest of what I have. I retired a while back so I have lots of time on my hands to poke around, pick up things."

"I'm sure you do," Gorodish said.

"Will you be at this number?"

"Yes. Call me back whenever you like."

"I think we ought to meet tonight, but I don't know exactly what time I'll be free. Just have the money ready and wait for my call."

Gorodish sat at the Steinway, his hands gripping his knees as he listened to the sound of stifled sobs coming from Alba's room.

After a while he rose and went into the kitchen. Opening the refrigerator door, he poured himself a large glass of milk and slowly drank it.

When his nerves had quieted he went into Alba's bedroom. She seemed calmer now. He did not put on the light, but sat down on the bed and began to caress her hair. At last she stopped crying.

Alba turned toward him. Gorodish held her tightly. "Why did you do that?" she asked.

"You know you're free to do whatever you want," Gorodish said softly, "only don't lie about it."

He lifted her and, holding her close, carried her to his king-sized bed.

"You didn't understand a thing, you asshole," Alba said coldly. "I know what you're thinking. Well, you can check, if you want. . . . *I* swam away from a sinking ship but *you*, you acted like a sailor on shore leave."

CHAPTER

8

THE SOUND OF THE TELEPHONE ringing tore Gorodish from Alba's embrace.

"Is that you?" Catfish asked nervously.

"Well, you're certainly up bright and early," Gorodish said sleepily as he glanced at the clock. It was five in the morning.

"I'm burned. They've spotted me."

"What are you talking about?"

"Someone tried to kill me last night. They tried to push me under a subway car at the Chatelet Métro station. It's a miracle I'm still alive."

"Who's that *someone*?"

"I don't know. I didn't see him. I just felt his hands on my back . . ."

"All right, calm down. Where are you now?"

"At home, Boulevard de Courcelles. They're after me. I have to see you right away. Do you have my money?"

"Yes."

"I can't stay here; they know where I live. I'll have to go

hide out in the Jura Mountains for a while. I've got family there."

"What's your address, and your apartment number?"

"Forty-six-*ter*, third floor, it's the apartment on the left."

"Stay put. I'm on my way."

"Listen, if something happens to me before you get here, I've sent my sister a letter with all the information. Her name's Juliette Dupraz. She lives at Twenty-two allée Carlo Lully, in Poissy. You give her the money; she'll give you the letter."

Gorodish jotted down the sister's address. "I'll be at your place in less than half an hour," he said.

He took his .45 from the armoire and loaded it. Then he dressed, picked up the envelope filled with money and left the apartment.

Gorodish found 46-*ter* easily enough but the street was crowded with cars and he was forced to double-park the station wagon. He was about to step out of the car when the front door of Catfish's building opened and a short, dark-haired man came out. The man looked around nervously, then walked quickly down the street.

Gorodish gave him enough time to reach the far corner before entering the building. He walked up to the third floor and was about to ring the bell when he saw that the door was ajar. The doorjamb was splintered, two black marks showing where the lock had been jimmied. Gorodish pulled out his .45 and cautiously entered the apartment, trying to sense what awaited him in the dark.

He could make out a heavy armchair covered in an ugly, flowered material, its armrests worn with use. Clothing lay piled on the seat. A large orange cat crouched on top of the clothes, its yellow eyes gazing indifferently at Gorodish. Pallid light from a streetlamp outside the window fell on the man's face. Gorodish switched on the overhead light. Catfish lay sprawled on his back, his throat cut, blood still spurting rhythmically from the carotid artery. Like all dying catfish, he was secreting large amounts of mucus from various parts of his body.

Gorodish realized that he had seen the killer. If only he had arrived a few minutes earlier, Catfish would still be alive. Suddenly, Gorodish remembered the man's sister: she was now his only remaining link to the mystery of Lola Black. He took out the slip of paper on which he had jotted down her address.

Gorodish had no trouble locating the small house in Poissy. Its yellow shutters were closed but he could see lights on inside. The alleyway was deserted. The rain had stopped and there was a hint of daylight in the cloud-covered sky. Dawn would soon be breaking.

The police would probably find Catfish's body soon. The man had undoubtedly included Alba-Info International's name and address in his letter to his sister. When the police came to see her she would tell them everything, unless, of course, her greed was stronger than her grief. Gorodish wondered if she had received the letter yet; there was a slim chance it would not arrive until this morning's mail.

He settled down to wait, knowing there was a risk that the dark-haired killer might show up before the postman did. It was a risk Gorodish had to take. The .45 lay on the seat beside him.

He listened to the sound of cars gliding by, their tires loud on the rain-damp street. Gorodish turned off the car's engine. The heater stopped blowing and cold air crept up his legs.

Day broke. The lights in the house went out and, a few moments later, the front door opened and a woman about fifty years old appeared. She glanced at her watch, then looked up and down the street. Gorodish was afraid she might walk toward him, but she turned and headed down toward the center of town.

Twenty minutes later he heard the creaking, metallic sound of a bicycle. Glancing into the rearview mirror, he saw a young black girl slip several letters into a neighbor's mailbox.

The girl pedaled past his car, stopped, searched through her heavy leather postal bag and pulled out a large manila envelope which she forced into the mailbox in front of Juliette Dupraz's house.

When the girl on the bicycle had disappeared down the street, Gorodish got out of his car, pushed open the yellow garden gate, opened the mailbox and retrieved the letter, relieved to see the right return address on the envelope.

He got back into his car and drove for several minutes before pulling over to the side of the road.

Impatiently, Gorodish tore open the envelope.

Paris, November 15

Dear Juliette,

You wouldn't believe what's been going on. When you get this letter I may be dead, but at least this is one time I'll be able to do something for you, something that'll prove that I'm not such a bad brother after all. I'm finally going to be able to take care of you, even if it's from the grave. And this is one time you can't be angry with what you were always calling my "stupid fishing."

A man will come to see you. He'll give you fifty thousand francs and you give him the enclosed envelope. Be very careful; don't let him take advantage of you and don't give him the envelope until after he gives you the money IN CASH. Don't worry. This is a perfectly legitimate business deal.

If it turns out that I'm still alive and that nothing's happened to me, you hold on to the envelope anyway. But don't open it. It's better if you don't know what's in it.

Henri

Gorodish glanced through the first letter and examined the enclosed envelope; "50,000 francs" was written across it in red ink. He opened the envelope.

Monsieur,

Here is the information we discussed about Lola Black, the singer. She is living with a man in the ruins of a riverfront café on an island in the Seine, across from Poissy. The island used to be called Ile aux Dames, but they've changed the name. The house is in the middle of the island and is hard to reach because the place is a jungle. There are no paths and the place is full of brambles and weeds and dead and fallen trees. It's the second island facing Poissy. The main island has a swimming pool, and there is a man who rents out boats and runs the refreshment stand. You'll have to shout for him to come get you. He's a nice old man and he knows me. Just tell him you're a friend of Monsieur Henri and he'll help you.

Catfish (Henri Dupraz)
46-ter *Boulevard de Courcelles*

Gorodish folded the letter and slipped it into his pocket. He was eager to find the island, but the entire situation had become more complicated now and he was afraid of making a wrong move. He would have to think of some way to get to the island without being seen. Showing up at eight o'clock on a rainy November morning and asking to rent a boat was not exactly subtle.

He decided to return to Paris and spend some time with Alba. It would give him a chance to think things through. Gorodish was hungry. He stopped at the first bakery he could find and bought croissants, savoring, in advance, his pleasure at awakening Alba.

• • •

Alba was already awake. Dressed in a pair of plain cotton pajamas she sat on the floor next to the piano, her eyes closed, her legs folded in lotus position. She did not move when Gorodish entered.

"Are you meditating?" he asked, smiling.

"I'm trying to get in touch with The Great Spirit of the Forest," Alba said seriously.

"That's a good idea. I think we'll be meeting him eventually."

"Oh?" Alba said. "Have you started meditating, too?"

"In my own way."

"Have you had a vision?"

"Better yet: a revelation. I see a small island in the Seine, and Lola and her lover hiding out there."

"That's wonderful!" Alba said. "See: the silent majority and the walking dead can't keep us from communicating with the Great Beyond."

"They might. The walking dead seem to be very handy with a knife; they've gutted Catfish."

"Really?" Alba said and unfolded her legs.

"I found him. They cut his throat."

"Poor man," Alba said, wrinkling her nose.

"Somehow, they managed to pick up his trail. I've got hold of the information he wanted to sell us but we have to plan our next move very carefully. The fact that they killed him proves he really did have something valuable."

"How far away is this island?" Alba asked.

"About an hour's drive."

"Aren't we going to take a look at it?"

"Of course we are, but we have to figure out how to get there without being noticed."

"I could go by myself. They wouldn't pay any attention to me. Oh, please, Serge, let me . . ."

"No. We have to convince them we're just a couple of innocent tourists looking around the place. There's a boat concession on the next island but it's November, and they've probably been hauled in for the winter. We'll have to come up with something better."

"I smell croissants."

"Let's have breakfast. Maybe we'll come up with an idea while we're eating."

"Was Catfish nice?"

"I didn't get a chance to know him, but this deal of his looks like a winner."

Gorodish sliced a croissant in half and smeared both sides with butter and honey. He watched as Alba, who was looking particularly childlike and innocent in her sky-blue pajamas, did the same.

"This weather sucks," Alba said sententiously, biting into the croissant and tossing back her long blond hair. Her breasts quivered. Gorodish looked away. Such strong emotion so early in the morning was too much for him.

"I wonder why she ran away," Alba said, thinking out loud. "Everything was going so well for her."

"We'll find out eventually."

"Of course Rimbaud deliberately disappeared, just when things were going well for him, too," Alba said, remembering what Gustave, her literature tutor had told her.

"Think up some way of getting to the island," Gorodish said.

"Is it very far from the riverbank?"

"I don't think so."

"We could wait until spring and swim over. Or we could go by boat. Or you could do a James Bond and parachute in, or rent yourself some underwater gear. Why don't you go play a Haydn sonata: that always cheers you up. And I'll take a long soak in my organic blue-grass body shampoo. That always helps cheer *me* up."

Gorodish's hands gently touched the keyboard. As the first notes of Beethoven's First Piano Sonata rose from the Steinway, he suddenly understood how the opening bars were meant to be played. He had been struggling with the opening of the piece for a long time now and this sudden revelation was merely further proof that great ideas take a long time to mature.

Alba's sudden appearance startled him. She stood naked in the doorway, her skin covered with green-tinged bubbles that slid down her body to pool on the carpet at her feet.

"Are you finished with your bubble bath?"

"No. I heard you playing and it was so beautiful I just had to make sure you hadn't snuck Alfred Brendel in here."

CHAPTER 9

GORODISH FINISHED PLAYING the Beethoven sonata. He remained seated at the piano for a long moment, a delicious feeling of lassitude filling his soul. Then, absolutely determined not to think of anything else for a while, he went into the kitchen and made himself a cup of coffee.

Gorodish took a few sips of the pure Colombian brew, then went to his room. Alba was in his bed.

"I was listening," she said. "Kiss me."

Gorodish bent over and placed his lips against his angel's warm, trembling mouth.

"How would you like to take a ride to Poissy?"

"I'd like that. Can I wear my veil, my alligator pumps, my jersey . . ."

"Jeans, boots and a turtleneck sweater."

Having decided it would be better to reconnoiter the island from the deserted stone quarry on the unpopulated side of the river, Gorodish drove across the Poissy bridge. Then they sneaked through the bushes to a spot directly across from Ile aux Dames. The island was nothing more than a long patch of ground covered with thick undergrowth and one lone, magnificent stand of trees. There was no sign of life, no dock, no place to land. Catfish had been right: the island was a jungle. The tawny waters of the Seine glided around that tiny, misplaced scrap of Africa.

"There are a lot of barges on the river," Gorodish said. "We'll wait for one to go by and use the engine noise for cover. Now, how would you like to come with me to the large island? There's a refreshment stand, and a man who rents out boats. The only thing is, I don't know what kind of story to tell him."

"Just say you're a teacher and you're going to bring your class here on an outing next spring. I'll pretend I'm one of your students. Ask him if he can rent you eight or ten boats and how much will it be, and like that. Remember to act nervous: most teachers live on their nerves all the time, trying to get through the semester and exams and inspectors' visits and supervisor's meetings, and all that business."

"Let's give it a try."

The boat was long and low; the sweep oar barely moved. The ferryman was tall and bony. He had a gray beard and deep-set eyes: Charon personified. Gorodish and Alba clambered into the boat.

They reached the larger island. "We don't usually have people out here this time of year," the ferryman said. He sounded suspicious.

A black-and-white mutt yapped at them from in front of the small, green-shuttered cabin. Next to the cabin stood a shed built of dark wood planking. A weathered blue sign hung from its roof: BOATS FOR RENT, the sign read; GARAGE.

Gorodish played his part to perfection. "We in the teaching profession," he said, "tend to plan ahead."

"So, you're a schoolteacher," Charon said. He sounded as if he didn't believe a word of it.

"Might we perhaps purchase a cup of coffee?"

"My wife'll make it."

They sat at a table covered in red-and-white-checked oilcloth. "This must have been a popular place for weekend outings before the war," Gorodish said in his most erudite manner.

"I was born on this island, and so was my father, and his father, and my great-grandfather before me," Charon replied.

"Then they must have known some of the famous artists of their day and seen many glamorous women."

"Meissonnier lived nearby, and there were plenty of pretty women used to come here, but now the whole river's polluted. They've fucked it up, turned it into a backwater. We can't even swim in the Seine anymore. I remember in the old days the women used to tuck up their long skirts and dabble their feet in the water, and there were small beaches all over the island and there was dancing. We had fish fries and more than thirty boats for rent. Those were great times. You couldn't find a boat free on the weekends and now there's only twelve left and hardly anybody comes here anymore. The Seine's a sewer. They all keep themselves so damn clean and fuck up everything around them."

"Don't get started, Ernest," his wife shouted from the kitchen, "you'll have another one of your attacks."

"Everything's 'amusing' these days," Charon continued. "Wine's 'amusing,' people are 'amusing,' even the river around here's 'amusing.' . . ."

"It seems to me it should be very pleasant here, in springtime and in the summer. Now, shall we discuss my little project? I'm planning a day outing, sometime before Easter break. I thought I'd bring my class to the river and show them what it used to be like: canoeing, a picnic. I have thirty-eight students. Now that de Maupassant is back in fashion young people rather like that sort of thing. Would you have enough boats to rent? Is there a spot nearby where we might picnic? I assure you it will not be a *Picnic on the Grass* as Manet painted it. . . ." Gorodish laughed, a perfect little tight-assed laugh.

"Thirty-eight students? That's a lot, but we'll manage somehow. You'll want the boats for the whole day?"

"Yes. It will be on a Thursday. Oh, that reminds me, our principal wanted me to ask if you might give us a discount on the price, especially since we'd be renting all your boats."

"I'll think about it."

"And would you know a quiet, isolated spot, a place where we could picnic comfortably? I thought, perhaps, that small island across from the quarry . . ."

"No good; it's full of quicksand. We had two people die there last year," Charon said darkly.

"Oh, dear," Gorodish said fearfully, "but I'm certain that people used to go there in the old days."

"No. There was never anything on that island."

"Are you positive? No refreshment stand? No dance pavilion? Nothing?"

"Nothing but dead people," Charon repeated, a touch of menace in his voice.

"Then we'll have to find someplace else," Gorodish sighed.

"There's time," Charon said. "Come back next week. I'll work out a price."

Two minutes later Alba and Gorodish had crossed the small inlet and were back on land.

"That is one scary guy," Alba said, summing up their visit.

Gorodish could feel an idea beginning to take root in his mind. They crossed back to the other side of the Seine, drove to Andresy and then turned downriver toward Conflans.

Swarms of barges were anchored along the riverbank. The barges seemed to shimmer in the gray light, their squat deckhouses silhouetted against the sky. Gorodish and Alba drove out of Conflans. There were fewer barges now. From time to time they could make out a tiny garden planted between the river and the deserted road.

"We have to find a way to reach the island from here," Gorodish said. "We'll be less conspicuous."

They drove past a café called The Old Barge. Next to it stood a marine supply store, motorboats on display in its front windows.

Gorodish made a U-turn. They entered the café and he ordered a café au lait for himself, bread-and-butter sandwiches and a glass of milk with grenadine syrup for Alba.

"Do you happen to know who owns those motorboats?" Gorodish asked the woman behind the counter.

"My husband. You looking for a boat? He just took in some nice ones in trade. Wait a minute, I'll call him."

The woman turned and shrieked something toward the back of the café. A person with particularly acute hearing might have deciphered the name "Raoul" hidden somewhere in the sound.

The Raoul in question appeared, his body stuffed into a pair of grease-stained blue overalls, his red hair waving wildly above a face that seemed eroded by rust-colored freckles. His answering cry matched his wife's in intensity.

"Whatisit?"

"This here lady and gennleman wanna buy a boat."

"I'll go get my keys."

He unlocked the marine supply warehouse. "You lookin' to buy a boat?"

"I wanted to rent a Bombard."

"I don't rent, I sell. And with the weather the way it is . . ."

"We're making a movie for television."

"Television?"

"Yes. We'll need a boat for a few days."

"I got a fifty-horsepower Mercury."

"Perfect."

"You the producer?"

"No. I'm his assistant."

"You do all the dirty work, right?"

"You got it," Gorodish replied.

"I bet the young lady's an actress, right? I think I seen her in something."

"That's possible," Alba improvised, her voice vibrating with dramatic disdain.

"What's your name?"

"Lola Morning."

The man examined her from head to toe, his eyes lingering longer on her top than her bottom.

"I think we can work something out," he said. "You want me to put it in the water for you?"

"Fine. Is the motor in good shape?"

"I worked on it myself."

"How much is it?" Gorodish asked, pulling a handful of money from his pocket.

"Two hundred francs a day, and you pay the gas."

"Much too expensive," Gorodish said.

"Very expensive," Alba agreed. "I only earn a hundred and fifty francs a day, myself."

Surprised, the man stared at Alba, then began rolling a cigarette in cheap yellow paper. "I know some guys'd pay more than that to get next to someone built as good as you. . . ."

Gorodish could feel Alba struggling to hold back a stinging reply.

"Okay," the man said, "I don't want you saying I overcharged you. Let's make it a hundred and fifty francs a day."

"I'll give you half now," Gorodish said, holding out the money."

"What's the name of this movie?"

"*On the River,*" Alba said. "It's based on a de Maupassant story."

"Oh, yeah, he's been getting a lot of publicity lately. Probably paid off all those people to mention his name all the time. Even heard the president say something about him in his last news conference. You let me know when they show your movie, maybe I'll watch it. But let me tell you, you'd never catch the head of the French Communist party hanging out with them goddamn television people, having his picture taken with them sellout actors; all those politicians thinking they can write, getting in tight with all that show-business crap. When will you be needing the boat?"

"Around ten tonight. Is that all right with you?"

"Where you planning to moor it for the night?"

"I'll bring it back, then pick it up again in the morning."

"I'll show you how to tie up. Hey," he said to Alba with what he obviously thought was a seductive smile, "how about giving me a autographed picture for over the bar?"

"Of course," Alba said, shifting her body into a starlet pose.

CHAPTER

10

DRESSED IN BLACK SLICKERS, Gorodish and Alba floated past the ruins of the old Poissy bridge. The water was dark and fathomless; only the town lights reflecting on its surface indicated that there was life here.

Trying to make as little noise as possible, Gorodish let the boat drift with the current.

He tied the boat to a tree branch and turned off the motor. "Now we wait for a barge," he said.

"I'm scared," Alba whispered.

"It'll be all right. We'll use the barge for cover and sneak over to that landing place we spotted a little while ago. I'll find the house. I promise you you won't have to wait very long, twenty minutes at the most. Just stay in the boat, keep the motor running and your eyes on the island. After twenty minutes, come and get me."

"Okay," Alba said in a melancholy voice, "but you be careful, Serge."

• • •

They could hear a barge approaching. It was almost invisible, its running light tracing a thin line across the night. Gorodish motioned to Alba and she shifted into reverse, practicing so that she would know what to do if the motor stalled. Maneuvering into position behind the long, rectangular shadow of the moving barge, she began to follow it.

They drew level with the Ile aux Dames and Alba turned in toward shore. Bits of shredded material hung from the lowest branches of the trees, deposited there by the high crests of winter.

The boat touched land. "Twenty minutes," Gorodish said, hugging Alba.

She could feel her body warming to his touch.

"If I see anything," she said, "I'll sound the marine horn three times."

"No. You do what we practiced: let it blast."

"It makes so much noise," she said. "The whole town will hear it."

"They won't pay any attention."

"All right. But you be careful."

Alba put the motor in reverse and the boat slid backward. She waved at Gorodish. He watched until she reached the far bank.

Gorodish moved far inland before turning on his pocket flashlight. He took the .45 from his belt and gripped it tightly. There was no path and he moved slowly, searching for an opening in the thick undergrowth, climbing over dead and fallen trees, through vegetation that looked petrified and menacing.

Gorodish tried to head directly toward the center of the island where Catfish had said the old café stood. He heard a night bird call. Despite the humidity, the fallen branches were dry and twigs cracked beneath his feet.

He saw a shadow to his right and turned the flashlight

on it, only to discover an old summerhouse in ruins, a beech tree growing up through its floorboards and roof.

Alba tied the boat to a bush and sat huddled in its bottom. She tried to peer through the dark, feeling very much alone, her mind filled with visions of everything that could go wrong. She began to tremble. Her hands tightened on the pocket flashlight and the marine horn.

She heard a noise. She was tempted to turn on the flashlight and shine it in the direction of the sound, but she did not dare.

Gorodish could sense a lightening of the space around him. He shut off the flashlight and walked forward blindly, moving as quietly as he could.

As his eyes became accustomed to the dark he could make out a low, massive shadow at the far end of the clearing. He was surprised not to see any lights and stopped again, trying to hear, to feel, what lay in the dark. He checked his watch. It was almost eleven o'clock: only five minutes left. Perhaps Lola and her lover were already asleep.

Quickly, Gorodish crossed the open terrain and approached the back of the house. The place looked like a cross between a trapper's cabin and a turn-of-the-century café. Under a lean-to he found a neatly stacked pile of logs covered with a tarpaulin.

Gorodish made his way around to the dilapidated front porch. Bushes poked through the rotten decking and he could see the faint gleam of four small windows.

He listened, hearing nothing but the creaking of the trees surrounding the cabin, then moved to a window, looked through it and saw a light rectangle floating within the gloom. It was a bed.

Alba watched as a large barge drew near, a series of waves preceding it, each wave higher than the one before. The long dark shape of the barge cut off her view of the island. She could hear voices and saw a faint glow against the sky. A German shepherd ran back and forth on deck; she could see its head and heard it bark three times. A voice shouted: "Quiet, Caesar!" and the dog fell silent. The barge moved on, the small boat in which Alba crouched rising and falling in its wake.

Alba looked at her watch again. Five more minutes. She shuddered and peered out into the night, trying to see the island.

Gorodish took a deep breath, pointed the flashlight into the room and turned it on. A bright circle of light tracked over a dresser, two photographs pinned to the wall and an unmade, empty bed. Gorodish pointed the flashlight toward the other bedroom: it, too, was empty. Now there was only the large room left, the one leading out onto the small, covered wreck of a porch.

Gorodish felt his muscles relaxing. There was a sign nailed to the doorjamb:

TRESPASSING FORBIDDEN. PREMISES BOOBY-TRAPPED.

Gorodish pressed his hand against the door. He hesitated a moment, then pushed. The door creaked as it opened. The house felt uninhabited. He examined the room carefully, running the beam of light across the walls before deciding it was safe to enter.

It had taken him longer than planned to explore the island: he would be late arriving at the pickup point. His skin prickling, Gorodish slowly shone the light at various parts of the room. The large space had been used as a combination living room, kitchen and dining area. The furniture was old: no two pieces matched and the cement floor was covered with threadbare throw rugs. A large rattan sofa stood between two armchairs; all the other furniture looked as if it had been built by someone who knew nothing about carpentry. The room resembled a set in a Grade B Western. Benches surrounded a table. There was a stove, two cans of butane gas and a half-filled larder. An odor of wood floated in the air; a pile of logs lay next to the stove. Gorodish walked over and touched the burners: they were cold.

In one corner he found a stack of paper plates and cups. There were also a dozen bottles of champagne and three covered dishes in which a few pieces of cheese were slowly turning to mold. A camp sink stood in the far corner; underneath it was a plastic water barrel fitted with a hand pump. Kerosene lamps stood on the table near the doorway through which he had entered. Prudently, Gorodish closed the door.

A kerosene lamp lay smashed next to a goatskin-covered couch. The two smaller rooms opened directly into the larger one: evidently they had been built to take advantage of the heat from the cookstove. Gorodish went into the first sleeping alcove. The bed was nothing more than a mattress on a rough wood frame. A pile of magazines lay on the floor, copies of *Astronomy*, the American journal, as well as a few copies of *People* magazine dating from the year before. A shelf held about fifty paperbacks, most of them detective novels.

Some orange crates were piled high with clothing: women's underwear as well as men's.

Gorodish entered the second sleeping alcove and examined the photographs pinned to the wall. Automatically, he noted the odor of sandalwood in the air and remembered the "biography" he had read: sandalwood was Lola's favorite perfume.

The first photo on the wall was of Arthur Rimbaud, the second was a postcard view of San Francisco. Gorodish pulled out the pushpins holding the photos to the wall, hoping to find something written on them that would give him a lead. There was nothing on the back of the postcard but the words CHAMBOLLE-MUSIGNY, and he recognized Lola's preference for the wines of Burgundy.

Among the worn clothing in the dresser drawers he found an Uher tape recorder and some tape cassettes. The labels had writing on them. Gorodish deciphered the violet scrawls: they were all titles of Lola's songs.

Gorodish went back into the main room. A plastic bottle standing next to the sink caught his eye: hair dye. The label read FLAME RED.

Maneuvering the boat back to the small island was easier than she had thought it would be. Alba checked her watch again: Gorodish was ten minutes late. She stared at the trees, listening for sounds, her imagination inventing disasters.

Suddenly she heard a dog bark and recognized the voice of Charon's mongrel. It sounded closer than it should have been: his house and the refreshment stand were on the far side of the larger island.

Alba conjured up visions of a boat hidden in the dark of the river, of Charon's emaciated body rowing toward her, of the mutt beside him in the boat. It would be an easy trip for him even at night.

Alone in the dark, Alba shivered. The dog barked again. Three times.

CHAPTER

11

SOMEWHERE, FAR OFF, A DOG barked. Gorodish pulled the cabin door closed and turned back toward the river.

Someone was moving heavily through the woods. Gorodish hid behind a tree and watched as a man walked up to the house. He tried to detect another presence hidden within the echo of the man's footsteps, but there was nothing.

Peering through the leafy trellis of dark branches, Gorodish saw the lights go on in the cabin. Quietly, he moved back toward them.

Charon was sitting at the table, eating cheese and drinking from a bottle of Burgundy.

When he finished he wiped his mouth on his sleeve, then picked up a kerosene lamp and went into one of the sleeping alcoves. Gorodish watched him remove the photograph and postcard from the wall, then rummage through the dresser drawers and take the tapes and tape recorder. Leaving the lamp in the bedroom, Charon carried the things he had found into the large room, packed them in a sail bag, then went back into the sleeping alcove and retrieved the lamp.

Charon wrapped what was left of the cheese in a piece of newspaper, stuffed three bottles of wine into the sail bag then walked over to the sink. He sniffed at the bottle of hair dye, rinsed it out at the faucet and slipped it into his pocket.

Gorodish waited until Charon left, then made his way back through the woods to the river.

Alba was pale and trembling. "I was so scared!"

"I found something interesting. And Charon showed up."

"Let's get out of here!"

"We have to wait for the next barge to pass."

"He'll see us."

"We'll hear him first."

The Old Barge café was deserted and silent. They anchored the boat at the pontoon dock and retrieved the station wagon from where they had hidden it.

Alba could not relax until they saw the lights of Paris. At that moment, even the most sinister parts of the city seemed like a haven of peace and security to her.

They entered the comforting surroundings of their own apartment, with its houseplants, its warmth, its light. Something had been slipped under their door: a fragile white rectangle lay on the red carpet. Alba picked up the envelope and opened it.

Gorodish was already running a bath.

"Serge! Serge!" Alba called, stunned by what the letter contained. Gorodish came hurrying into the room. "Look at this: it's crazy! Phil Mann's sent me a translation of a letter that was published in the *Washington Post* the day before yesterday!"

Gorodish quickly scanned the note Phil Mann had enclosed with the translation.

"Hey, Alba, haven't heard from you. I'll be at *les Nouvelles littéraires* tomorrow morning. Thought you'd like to see this. Phil."

"After a preliminary investigation, the *Washington Post* has decided to publish the following text. The letter, received yesterday, purports to be from rock star Lola Black, whose death was reported last June. Despite the findings of a California coroner's jury, which declared Miss Black to have died of unknown causes, the *Washington Post* is convinced of the authenticity of this letter. After close inspection, three members of Miss Black's former band have identified the handwriting as being that of the rock star. Mr. Anthony Nash, Detroit industrialist, and the singer's father, has refused to identify the handwriting as being that of his daughter but this afternoon posted a reward of one million dollars for information leading to her return. A police investigation is under way to trace the origins of the letter, which was postmarked Detroit, Michigan. Anyone with information regarding the whereabouts of Lola Black is asked to telephone this newspaper at the following 800 number. . . ."

I AM ARTHUR RIMBAUD

Autumn already, but why mourn the eternal sun when we are seeking the heavenly light, far from the season's dying?

Autumn. Our boat floats on frozen fog, turns toward poverty port, the enormous city with its spotted sky of fire and mud. Oh, the rotting rags, the rain-drenched bread; head spinning, a thousand loves have crucified me. Will it never end, that ghoulish queen reigning over a million souls and dead bodies waiting to be judged?

Sometimes I see endless beaches in the sky, white with celebrating crowds. A great golden ship above me, its rainbow banners waving in the morning breeze. And I created every festival, every triumph, every play: I tried inventing new flowers, new stars, new flesh, new tongues. I dreamed of supernatural powers, and found that I must bury imagination, memories and all that's left of fame: a fitting end for a bard who simply got carried away!

One summer night Rimbaud fucked my soul in the woods of Big Sur. He is The Great Spirit of the Forest, silence and the trees.

My brothers, Mexico Flat, Tommy Bonaparte, Sitting Bull Plastic, I love you all in the far-off clouds of music.

I send this message of love to the world, saying, simply: I've found the silence. I am Arthur Rimbaud. See my eyes captured in his pale face.

Oh, my brothers, do not fear the silent legions for purity will reduce them to ashes. Yes, I am an animal, forever lost to your light!

Do I still know Nature? Do I know myself? . . . *No more words.* I bury the dead in my belly. Cries, drums, dance, dance, dance, dance! With the coming of the white man I can no longer tell when I will sink into nothingness.

Hunger, thirst, cries, dance, dance, dance, dance!

Lola, Aden-Eden

"That's so beautiful. It must be from Lola," Alba said. "Remember, I told you she'd probably just gone away like Rimbaud did? She's incredible. And we're terrible, trying to force her back to a way of life that no longer has any meaning for her."

Gorodish placed his hands on either side of Alba's face and gazed down into her eyes. "We have to keep looking," he said. "Maybe things aren't what they seem. Maybe they aren't the way they're being presented to the public."

"Why not?" Alba asked innocently.

"Don't you think it strange that Lola felt she had to tell the whole world she's found peace? She was safe: everybody thought she was dead. Now everyone will be trying to find her: her father, the record companies, her agent, the IRS, her fan clubs. People will do anything to get hold of that million dollars."

"Oh," Alba said, "I forgot about the million dollars." Her smile had an edge to it. Gorodish watched her mull over the questions he had raised.

"It's strange," she said after a while, "but I'm not sleepy anymore."

"I'm going to take a bath," Gorodish announced.

"You know what I want to do?" Alba said coaxingly. "While you're in the bath, I'd like to cook up a bunch of French fries. Then we could lie in bed and eat them with loads of ketchup."

"Need any help slicing the potatoes?"

"No. I can do it myself."

It was two in the morning. Gorodish and Alba lay in bed, the covers pulled up to their chins, a tray holding a mountain of fries, a glass of wine, a carton of milk and a bottle of ketchup on the blanket between them. Their fingers were greasy and they took great care not to smear the photographs and newspaper articles spread across the bed.

"Do you think Charon's in on it?" Alba asked.

"Yes. If he wasn't, he wouldn't have tried to stop us from going to Ile aux Dames."

"Do you think he knows it's Lola Black?"

"Of course. He's probably in it for the money. He takes care of the day-to-day logistics, acts as point man, observation post and clearinghouse. Catfish shouldn't have trusted him. One thing I know for certain: it was Catfish's poking around that convinced Lola and her friend they'd been spotted."

"You think the old man killed Catfish?"

"No. That was a professional hit."

"Do you think they're still hiding in the old man's house?"

"It'd be too dangerous. I searched the cabin thoroughly and they left in a hurry. They didn't bother to take anything with them and there was a broken lamp. And Lola's dyed her hair red. Charon has to know where they are: he came to the cabin and took some of the things they'd left behind, and he tried to get rid of any evidence that could prove they'd been there. He's either keeping Lola's things at his place and her lover will come for them, or he's going to take them to where she's hiding. The worst possible situation for us would be if Charon kept Lola's things for a while before giving them back to her. We have time for a few hours' sleep before we go back to Poissy. I want to set up a surveillance on Charon."

"But he knows us."

"He's seen me, but as far as you're concerned, he's only seen a little schoolgirl. He'll never recognize you if you wear your black jersey dress, your high heels and that hat and veil."

They finished the French fries. Alba put the tray on the floor next to the bed while Gorodish set the alarm clock for five.

"May I spend the night with you?" Alba asked.

Gorodish did not answer. He merely turned off the light and took her in his arms. Alba felt as if she were a boat floating down a slow, warm river.

CHAPTER 12

GORODISH PARKED AS CLOSE AS he dared to Charon's island, took out a pair of binoculars and aimed them at the house. It was early but there was light behind the lace curtains and he could see someone moving back and forth, although he could not make out who it was.

Wrapped in a plaid blanket, Alba, Queen of the Night, napped, her head pressed against Gorodish's shoulder. Her hat and veil waited on the backseat.

The asphalt road seemed to undulate; details of its surface slowly became visible. For a few seconds, in the quickly changing light of dawn, the road resembled a pathway strewn with gray pearls. The sky turned white.

At exactly nine o'clock the door of the refreshment stand opened and Charon appeared, wearing a sheepskin vest against the cold. Gorodish watched him through the binoculars. Charon was holding a package tied with string. He walked briskly down the small path to the dock where his boat lay moored.

"He's carrying a package," Gorodish said to Alba. "Get ready."

Alba put on the hat and adjusted the veil. The world became a series of tiny squares that moved and trembled before her anxious eyes.

"Be careful. One slip and we'll lose him. There's no telling what he's going to do: take a bus, or a taxi, or walk. . . ."

Charon crossed the river, moored his boat on the far bank and climbed the steep stairs leading to the street. Gorodish's instincts had been right: Charon checked the area, turned left, walked up the quays of the Seine and disappeared around a corner.

"We can't follow him in the car: it's a one-way street going in the wrong direction. You follow him, but keep your distance. I'll go on ahead and pick him up at the far end of the quays."

"What do I do if I lose you?"

"Just keep going. But be careful: don't take any chances."

"Okay," Alba said. "I'm not afraid."

Gorodish kissed her, then watched her walk away.

Alba turned the corner and saw Charon moving quickly up the street. She crossed over to the other side, as she had seen actors do in movies. Charon was directly ahead of her now. A wisp of fog rose from the Seine.

The old man limped: his left leg was shorter than his right. Alba followed Charon the entire length of the quay. Luckily, he did not look back and did not turn into a side street.

Gorodish took a seat in a café, hoping that the man would not spot him watching the street. Soon Charon came into view, blending into the growing crowd of passersby.

Gorodish could not help smiling as he caught sight of Alba on the far side of the street. The old man was heading for the center of town. She could follow him more safely now.

Gorodish fell in behind Alba. It was probably a market day in Poissy: the street was packed with people, many of them carrying shopping baskets.

Afraid of losing Charon in the crowd, Alba hurried to catch up with him. Her heart was beating furiously and she could feel the excitement building inside her. For a fraction of a second she locked glances with a man. He stopped in his tracks, then began following her.

Damn! Alba thought.

The man grabbed her arm. "Tell me I'm not hallucinating," he said with a slick smile.

She did not react. "Let me buy you a cup of coffee," he insisted. "Give me just five minutes of your time . . ."

Alba kept her eyes on Charon. The man holding her arm looked like the sort who would not give up easily. She tried to think of something to say but was afraid he would take even a cutting remark as an invitation. His type usually considered a sneer progress, an insult victory. On the other hand, if she said nothing the idiot would keep up his rap forever.

Gorodish watched the scene unfold, unable to interfere, cursing himself for his helplessness, knowing that this interruption might ruin everything.

Undiscouraged by her silence, the creep kept running his mouth. "I can tell you're not one of those uptight chicks who's afraid of strangers."

That did it.

"A thousand francs an hour," Alba said, "and you pay for the hotel room."

"A thousand francs . . ." the creep croaked and stopped in his tracks.

Gorodish crossed the street and walked past them. The man was looking very unhappy. Gorodish wondered what the little she-devil had said to him.

Alba hurried to catch up with Charon.

It dawned on Gorodish that the old man was heading for the post office. It was all up to Alba now: if she didn't pull it off they would be reduced to using violence.

Alba followed Charon into the huge, crowded post office. Charon was holding the package tightly under his arm, the address hidden against his body.

He took a place in the parcel post line. STAMPS SOLD HERE said a sign above the window. Keeping her face averted, Alba searched through her pockets, found a few crumpled bills, pulled them out and began counting them. There were two people ahead of Charon. He was holding the package even more tightly now. Alba considered crouching down to tie her shoe, then remembered she was wearing pumps. Maybe he wouldn't notice. She examined the package carefully and realized there was nothing she could do, no subterfuge that would work. Her one chance was to try to read the address when Charon placed the package on the marble counter at the window, or while he was gluing on the stamps. She prayed the postal clerk would not turn out to be one of those helpful types who pasted on the stamps for the customer.

At last it was Charon's turn, but he was so tall and the sheepskin vest so large that she could not see past him. Panic.

"I want to send it registered mail," Charon said.

"You can't send registered mail to a post office box," the clerk said, weighing the package.

Alba hesitated. She could, on some pretext or other, barge up to the window, demand information from the clerk and sneak a look at the package. But Charon was no fool and she might ruin everything. Behind the clerk a dozen or more parcels lay on the floor. Something clicked in Alba's mind. There was a good chance that Charon's package would wind up on the pile, too, then all she would have to do is read the name of the city.

She could hear stamps being thumped onto cardboard. The package soared through the air and landed on the floor. Charon turned to his right and walked away and Alba moved up to the window.

"A roll of one-franc stamps, please," she said.

The clerk fumbled through the stamp drawer. Alba concentrated on the package. The writing was upside down, but she managed to make out

CANNES 06400

A gust of excitement rose from her belly and settled in her head. She paid for the stamps, waited a moment inside the door to give Charon time to move away from the post office, then walked out into the street, her step lively, assured, triumphant.

Charon had disappeared in the crowd. Alba searched for Gorodish but could not find him. She looked for the station wagon and suddenly saw it coming down the avenue. Gorodish opened the door and Alba climbed in.

"Got it!"

Gorodish let out a sigh of relief.

"It's a post office box in Cannes."

"Those bastards, they're really being careful!"

"I take it we're going to follow the package?" Alba asked.

"Exactly."

"I've never seen the Mediterranean," Alba said dreamily. "When do we leave?"

"Late this afternoon. But we have plenty of time: the package won't get there for two days."

"This is going to be fun," Alba said, a sunny smile on her face.

CHAPTER 13

ALBA PUT *FIRES* ON THE TURN-table. "Serge, may I call Phil?"

"Of course. Just don't tell him we're going to Cannes; you can never tell."

Alba dialed *les Nouvelles littéraires* and, after some confusion about correct extension numbers, managed to get through to Phil Mann. "Hi, this is Alba."

"Did you get my letter?"

"Yes. Listen, I thought I ought to tell you: I'm living with somebody."

"That's okay. We can still see each other."

"Sure, we can. Listen, I'm going away for a few days. I'll call you when I get back, okay?"

"Okay. And if I hear any news about Lola I'll keep it for when you get back. Strange, you getting interested in her just when she turned up again. I think she really did write that letter, don't you? My next TV program's about her. Try to catch it next Saturday. I've got hold of some film clips nobody's ever seen."

"I'll watch it. See you later."

As night fell the station wagon rolled swiftly down Hustler's Highway aka The Sunshine Road aka the route leading from Paris to the French Riviera. Each summer millions of suckers joined the traffic crawling down this same road, choking back their impatience and irritation as they choked down the lousy ham sandwiches sold at every roadside café. The more prudent travelers brought along their own supplies of food, as if practicing for the day in the near future when they might be forced to carry supplies of gasoline, too. Perhaps, by that time, Science would have learned to turn milk into methane, and the herds of cows that browsed along the route would no longer be safe.

Alba felt her soul being swept clean by the oncoming headlights. She relaxed, enjoying the magic of the road, the air whistling along the side of the car, the long, bare ribbon of empty highway. There was nothing here to distract a driver. By concentrating on the abstract design of asphalt lanes and yellow stripes, Alba managed to attain a meditative state. It seemed to her as if the car were standing still, the road beneath them unreeling like some huge slidewalk.

"What are you thinking about?" Gorodish asked softly.

"I was trying to make up a sentence using only words beginning with the letter *s*."

"Let's hear it."

"Wait a minute: I have to polish it a little bit more."

Silence.

Alba turned toward Gorodish. His profile was silhouetted against the humid gray film coating the inside of the car window. Passing headlights illuminated individual droplets on the glass, turning them into flashing pixels of light against the night sky. Alba took a deep breath and began to chant, phrasing the sentences as if reciting a poem:

"Some sad September Saturday, Sid the Stableboy, a Saturnian Siamese swordsman sans skills, succumbed to Sally, supreme strumpet, sensual slut, sleek with salient symmetry. Stupefying Sally sweltered in her sweat suit, singing a samba as she smoked a synthetic stimulant surreptitiously stolen in Sausalito. Sally swiveled on the seedy sedan seat, smiled saucily as Sid scuffed his shoe, snarled, scowled and stormed the sexual stronghold. Self-control! Self-indulgence! Self-satisfaction! Satiation!"

Gorodish smiled.

"I want to break in my new cigarette holder," Alba said. "Do you have a king-size cigarette?"

"I thought you'd bought some."

"I bought a pack of Kools because I like the name, but I don't want to open them."

Alba smoked half a cigarette, puffing the smoke toward the windshield and then crushing out the butt in the car's ashtray.

"When will we get in touch with Lola's father?"

"We'll wait awhile to make absolutely sure we know where she is."

"What's the exchange rate for the dollar?"

"Around eight francs, give or take a few centimes."

"Not too shabby," Alba said.

They stopped at Avallon, a name well known in the history of restaurants and music.

In honor of the occasion, Alba lowered her veil. They made their way through a labyrinth of food, filling their plates, Alba taking salad, cold roast beef and three napoleons, Gorodish ordering country ham, French fries, a glass of beer and, in homage to Lola, some goat cheese.

Alba asked the waiter to put the napoleons in the microwave oven for a few seconds, just to see what would happen.

• • •

The road undulated through the night, meandering like a river, ever more deserted now, ever more beautiful. Alba was filled with joy. Her mind roamed as she dreamed of the sea and a deep blue, star-filled sky: the two always seemed to go together. The landscape, dimly seen through the car windows, moved her. Small shivers ran through her body and she fantasized herself nude, suspended in space, carried aloft on a gossamer wave of pleasure. Heat filled her body and she felt herself becoming as fluid as music.

"Stop the car," she said, her voice trembling.

The sound of the motor faded. She saw the white and yellow lines change into the grassy edge of the road, the highway disappear behind its border of trees.

Gorodish turned off the headlights. Alba lowered the window to hear the breeze. The station wagon seemed to quiver with energy.

Gorodish took Alba's face in his hands and kissed her warm, trembling eyelids, kissed her temples and her golden hairline. His lips touched her impatient mouth and he drank in the perfumed honey of her breath.

Alba opened her jacket, her cotton blouse, offering her breasts to Gorodish's lips. She held him tenderly, feeling as if the road had stopped for them in this place, as if time had been suspended here. And they sat in the car, not moving, their arms around each other, listening to the thundering pulse of the forest.

CHAPTER

14

THERE WAS A KNOCK AT THE door. A chambermaid entered, carrying a large tray which she placed on the table.

"Could you please draw the drapes and open the windows?" Gorodish asked, slipping a folded ten-franc note into her hand. He sat up in bed. Golden sunlight crept into the room.

"Oooh, too fine," Alba exclaimed. "It's so beautiful! I was so tired last night, I didn't really get a good look at it."

"I'll say it's too fine," Gorodish said, amused. "We're at the Martinez Hotel."

Alba went over to the French windows. "I can hear the sea. And there're palm trees down there."

She went out on the balcony, remaining there for a good three minutes. Gorodish contemplated his angel, seeing her body in the transparent nightgown, incorporeal, unreal, her hair blowing in the wind.

"The air's so clean. It smells of sea and pine trees," Alba shouted.

Suddenly she turned and, laughing, threw herself at Gorodish. It could have been a mattress commercial: the bed took the shock and bounced back.

She beat him up, she rolled around with him under the covers, she tried to kick him out of bed, she smothered him under a soft pillow. At last, victorious, she installed herself across his naked chest, immobilizing his arms with her knees.

Gorodish could feel the subtle warmth of her pubis pressing against his solar plexus.

Laughing, Alba rose and brought the breakfast tray to the bed. She placed it between them, sat down facing Gorodish and crossed her legs. He leaned forward to kiss her before pouring the coffee.

There was absolutely no chance the package would arrive before the next day, yet Gorodish took up a vigil in front of the post office and tried to memorize the face of everyone who entered.

Alba prepared herself for her first day in Cannes as if planning an invasion or performing a ritual. At last she was ready. She sauntered across the lobby and a dozen men went into orbit.

Alba had removed the veil from her hat so that nothing would stand between her and the city. The first item on her agenda was to choose a direction in which to walk. She decided to turn to the right for a preliminary inspection of the area: she could always retrace her steps and go left instead.

The Promenade seemed a likely target. Beyond the Promenade, beyond the sandy beach, the tide seemed to be rising, breakers rolling in as if hurrying to watch the shadowy angel stroll past. The sea here was greedy, the annual film festival not enough to sate its appetite: and here was another beauty, come to greet it out of season.

The sun broke through. Alba stretched like a cat, her stride lengthening, becoming more fluid, taking on a tropical rhythm.

The landscape followed her progress, palm branches turning

as she passed. A hundred yards up the avenue she caused an accident. It wasn't her fault: the drivers should have been watching where they were going, not watching Alba out for her morning walk.

Alba's mind was in the clouds: she had no idea of the havoc she was causing.

Two zealous cub reporters, sent to Cannes by a center-left-liberal-intellectual weekly magazine to take a poll on attitudes toward marriage (ugh, yuk, gross), their effect on the gross national product and the impact of the government's latest slogans on the working class, saw that sublime shadow appear on the horizon. Grabbing pens and questionnaires, they descended on Alba like birds of prey in heat.

"Do you have a minute?"

"Yes," Alba said with her loveliest smile. She was not about to discourage the first two guys trying to pick her up in this incredibly beautiful beach town.

"We're taking a poll for a magazine . . ."

"Which magazine?"

"*The New Observer.* How old are you?"

"Seventeen," said the other cub reporter, impatiently, "eighteen, nineteen, who cares? Are you married?"

"No."

"Do you have any children?"

"No," Alba said. This was fun.

"How many children do you want to have?"

"Fifteen, twenty."

The two Observers laughed. "Would you like a drink?"

"Okay. By the way," Alba lied, "I'm sixteen."

They crossed the boulevard and sat down at a sidewalk café.

"You want a pastis?"

"Too fine," said Alba.

They yammered for over an hour while Alba downed three pastis. Then, sadly, the two Observers went back to their poll.

Alba decided to walk down the Croisette. It took her a minute or two to realize that the sea was no longer horizontal. She was smashed.

Alba burst into wild laughter. People stared at her and wondered if she was high on drugs.

It occurred to her that a little exercise might do her good. She jogged a hundred yards, then remembered she was wearing high heels which wasn't making running any easier.

Alba slowed to a walk. Her cheeks were hot, her mind mush, her body floating and diffuse. She decided that as long as she stayed in Cannes she would drink three pastis a day. She was in ecstasy. The city was hers: there was no one to challenge her claim to it, no other star in sight. It was a sublime moment. Alba sighed, breathing in the sea air.

The wind didn't seem all that strong, but the palm trees were beginning to bend. Alba tried to make plans for the evening, forgetting that Gorodish had to be at the post office before it opened in the morning.

She checked the circuits in her microcomputer, checked the state of her random access memory, checked her inertial guidance system and started up her ion drive. There was just time enough for a rainbow to form and she was gone, beyond the galaxy. She began with a visit to an unknown planet, landing on a soft steel desert swept by magic winds. She heard the Gibsonian and Fenderian voice of Lord Arcos, Emperor of the Underbelly of the Universe, saying, "Are you all right, Alba?"

"Perfec. How 'bout chu?"

"Come on, let's go back to the hotel."

They walked hand in hand and the desert beneath their feet bloomed with extraordinary flowers. From time to time she peered up at her handsome guide, but it was only when he led her into the lobby of the Galactic Palace of Arcos that she realized he looked a hell of a lot like Gorodish.

CHAPTER 15

ONE DAY FOR NOTHING: COUNT it off. Happily, there was the evening, a candlelit dinner in the proper setting to display Alba's flawless, uncut beauty.

They awakened to a perfect morning, langourous, as usual. Then, halving the beat, made it to the post office in time.

The next day they waited until four in the afternoon before the twitchy, dark-haired man showed up driving an enormous chunk of Detroit iron, a white Chevy Impala with red leather upholstery.

Gorodish waited in the station wagon.

Jean-Michel Diamant came out of the post office. He was not carrying the package. Obviously, he was too antsy to wait in line. Jumping lithely into the white whale, thereby displaying a certain familiarity with the style and technique of street cruising, he turned on the motor, pulled away from the curb and glided down the Croisette, followed, at a reasonable distance, by Gorodish and Alba.

PAN past the palm trees to a point where we SEE the road to Nice, the one running parallel to the railroad tracks.

Gorodish drove along behind him, not pushing the station wagon. The fish was sounding: might as well give him some line.

To Gorodish's relief, the trip was a short one. The white monster turned off the beautiful road, went up a hill, drove through a heavy iron gate and stopped in front of an incredible mansion built in the purest turn-of-the-century rococo style. The house was a veritable Moorish palace, with terraces, lush gardens and high, ogival windows. A tycoon's folly, it was slightly time-battered, yet still sumptuous, with sea-vu, all mod. convs. Gorodish was tense: everything was falling into place, almost.

"Not a bad place for a hideout," Alba said. "You think they'll ask us in?"

"We'll ask ourselves in," Gorodish said. "We'll come back tonight and have a look around."

"Are we dressing?"

"How would you like to have lunch in Vence?"

"Too fine," Alba said and draped herself across the car seat like a movie star.

Jean-Michel Diamant walked into a large sitting room that looked as if ten plasterers, and as many cabinetmakers, all of them high from sniffing glue, had spent years fulfilling the Queen of Sheba's every whim. Everything, the furniture, the piles of cushions, the colored lights, added to the atmosphere of Byzantine delirium.

There was also a panoramic view of the sea.

Lola dominated the room. She lay sprawled on a pile of cushions, listening to the latest Motorhead album playing on a stereo which was still in its packing case. The speakers were shaking so hard that Jean-Nasty-Michel was forced to turn the volume down. He had already misplaced his conscience: he had absolutely no wish to lose his hearing, too.

The telephone rang. Jean-Michel frowned. Nobody knew this number. But he answered the telephone anyway.

"This is Luc."

"How's it going, Papa?"

"Did you get the tapes?"

"Not yet. I was at the post office this morning, but . . ."

"Watch your step, son; I'm worried. I have a bad feeling about this one. Maybe you ought to go back to America; you were doing all right there."

"Don't worry, Papa; you know I always manage somehow."

"Listen, I think someone's after you. There was a man here the other day, said he was a teacher, but he looked about as much like a teacher as you and I do. Too interested in the island. It got me thinking. He tried to run a scam on me; it didn't feel right so I checked him out. A phony."

"Don't worry, Papa. Was he a big guy, kind of husky, had a little blond chick with him?"

"How'd you know?"

"I saw them following me a while ago. I'm going to set up a little diversion, just in case they come around here."

"Are you sure you can handle it, son?"

"Don't worry. I'll call you when it's over, tell you how it went."

The prodigal son hung up. He had a sudden urge to clap his hands, just to see if a harem would appear. Unfortunately, there was no harem handy.

"What did he say?" Lola asked.

"Nothing, baby."

The Yank from Poissy went over to the refrigerator and mixed himself a Monaco: beer and grenadine syrup. Then he rejoined Lola, his body sinking into the cushions of a chair large enough to hold all the Sheikhs of Araby.

• • •

Gorodish and Alba watched the pink marble mansion liquefy and melt into the fiery sea. They waited. The sky was deep blue, already sporting a few stars spotted between currant-colored clouds.

Time passed. At last, it was night. The Moorish windows were ablaze with light.

"Are we going to wait long?" Alba asked. She would rather have gone in the front door.

At eleven they were surprised to see HER, Lola, come out the front door and walk down the stairs. Her hair was red. She was wearing blue jeans and a fringed vest. She got into the Chevy and took off in a cloud of dust.

Gorodish followed as she headed straight for the Croisette and parked in front of the Palais des Festivals. Gorodish had no trouble finding a parking space.

Before getting out of the Chevy, Lola hid her eyes behind a large pair of black-and-white sunglasses. Then she walked up a side street leading toward the Rue d'Antibes. She entered the Quickie Bar, a place catering to a strange mixture of rockers, semi–Hell's Angels, innocents and tourists, none of whom came there in search of sparkling conversation. The decibel level was high enough to cause brain damage in the most fanatic rocker.

Gorodish and Alba waited until Lola found an empty booth, then followed her into the bar and seated themselves in a corner. There was about as much light as in a rat's nest and the dark leather decor was not designed to make visibility any better.

Lola remained there two hours, bathing in the blast of music. A stud wearing a leather jacket, his nose underlined by a cute little mustache, stopped at her table. It was entirely possible that they spoke; it was for sure that they could not hear each other.

Five minutes later they left the bar together.

Back up the Croisette, lights, palm trees silhouetted against a metallic blue sky.

They got into the Chevy, cruised around awhile and then headed back toward Nice.

Lola drove past the sultan's palace and kept going.

The port at Antibes, cool in the tender night, and on toward the rock-covered beach.

The Impala moved silently. Baie des Anges, Bay of Angels, deserted now, and quiet, an occasional car passing and the white whale gliding over the stony beach as if determined to swim to North Africa, its red taillights suddenly invisible, then visible again.

The Impala parked between two large concrete pilings facing the dark sea.

Gorodish shut off the headlights and parked the station wagon far enough from the Impala so as not to be seen. He opened the glove compartment, took out a pair of binoculars and aimed them at the white whale.

The windows were open but it was impossible to make out the people in the car, other than to see that they were wound around each other.

"There's only one pair," Alba complained. Gorodish handed her the binoculars.

"I can't see anything. Just something going up and down and something else that looks like a boot."

They waited a half hour, Gorodish remembering "Letter to No One."

> We didn't say a word, the space between us was fluid and glittering with gold dust. We walked to where you'd parked your car, that old blue Ford that'd covered so much territory, the universe reflected in its corroded chrome, its seats gleaming under the streetlights. You turned on the radio. Billie Holiday was singing "My Man." I watched the moonlight gleaming in your tears.
>
> When it was over you turned off the radio and said, real low, as if you were talking to heaven, "Billie."
>
> We rode for hours, we didn't care where we were going.

You stopped the car in the desert, with that great milky light overhead, and you told me to kiss your hair. I kissed your hair and we looked at each other and took off our jeans. Your bikini panties were green. We made love while a Mexican crossing the desert on foot watched us, his eyes shining under the brim of his hat.

"I don't have a hat," Gorodish said through clenched teeth.
"Kiss me," Alba said.

Lola drove back to Cannes and dropped off the stud near the Quickie Bar. Then she headed back in the direction of the Moorish monument moored above the Med.

CHAPTER 16

ALBA HAD LOST HER APPETITE for breakfast. There was a knot in her throat: something about Gorodish's plan was making her very unhappy.

"There's got to be some other way to do it," she said.

"No; it's perfect. This way there'll be no risk when we meet Lola. You'll see, it'll work . . ."

"Sure it will: for you. But I'll be sitting there like an asshole waiting for you to come back from wallowing with her. I don't know if you've noticed, but she wasn't exactly interested in discussing philosophy . . ."

"That's because nobody knows who she is. It'll be different with me."

"Sure it will," Alba said with tears in her eyes.

Gorodish tried to take her in his arms, but she pushed him away.

"Come on," Gorodish said, "this is just one more hard part to get through."

"Our lives seem to be filled with hard parts to get through," Alba said. "I think I'll pass on this one."

"Let's go," Gorodish said calmly, "we'll take a walk and buy the things we'll need for tonight."

"All right," said Alba, determined not to let him see her rage.

They left the hotel and stopped in a nearby bar for a pastis, just to quiet their nerves. Then they headed for the Rue d'Antibes where Alba had noticed a store selling jeans.

She floated on a small cloud of pastis, nothing as spectacular as the day before yesterday, but delicious just the same.

"I hope she shows up tonight so we can get it over with."

"Don't think about it," Gorodish said. "Concentrate on shopping."

They walked into Ali Baba's treasure cave. It smelled of leather. There was leather everywhere: real leather, good leather, used leather, braided leather, studded leather, Western leather, Hell's Angels' leather, disinfected leather for the squeamish and boots with decorated tips and heel ornaments. It was almost, but not quite, Mexico.

There was no problem transforming Alba into a rocker: the uniform looked tough on her, black boots, black leather pants, a used pilot's jacket with many air miles on it, its woolly skin turned inside out (the better to rub up against your T-shirt, my dear) and a studded leather belt to pull the whole outfit together. Plus, little pink sunglasses with silver glitter frames, a TED NUGENT LOVES ME button (bend over, let me hone the cutting edge of the New Music on the razor strop of your heart). Okay, so it wasn't exactly black jersey, alligator pumps and a hat with a veil, but it wasn't exactly shit, either. It had a *je-ne-sais-quoi,* a certain charm, a definite sensuality. Alba moved, she rocked, she hippety-hopped. She helped Gorodish put together his own outfit and added the final touch, a leather aviator's helmet dating back to 1920: divine! He had a perfect face for secondhand clothes. Alba almost stuck a LOLA button on him, but decided not to push it.

Gorodish handed the salesman thirty francs and asked that their civilian clothes be sent to the Martinez Hotel. The wimp almost swallowed his gum.

They hit the street and caused an instant scandal.

"Shame! Disgusting! Do you see what's roaming the streets these days? This used to be a decent neighborhood. And she's so young, too."

They passed the test: they hadn't gone a hundred yards before a cop car pulled them over.

"Let's see some identification."

They showed some identification.

First cop: "Where are you staying here in Cannes?"

Gorodish: "The Martinez Hotel."

Second cop: "Watch it, asshole, we don't take that kind of shit from scumbags like you."

Gorodish: "Room one thirty-two. Check it out."

The cop was silent for a moment. He glanced at his partner who, after thoroughly inspecting their papers, said, "Everything seems in order. They're not *real* scumbags."

First cop: "Please accept our apology, sir, but with all the real scumbags on the street these days we occasionally mistake fake scumbags for the real thing."

"That's quite all right," said Gorodish in a conciliatory tone.

The two cops took a step backward, bowed, bowed again, backed up and, bowing all the way, got back into the patrol car. Disappointed, the crowd dispersed.

"There's still something missing," Alba said. "I have an idea." She took Gorodish by the hand and dragged him into a pet store.

"May I help you?" twittered the old bird behind the counter.

"Perhaps," Alba said icily. "I would like a collar for a bitch."

"What breed?"

"Oh, the usual thing."

The collars were hanging on a rack. "Would you care to pick one? We also carry choke chains for obedience training. . . ."

"I won't need that until later tonight," Alba said with a menacing look at Gorodish.

She buckled a collar around his throat. It was perfect, and infinitely cheaper than a little something from Cartier's. Gorodish handed over the bread and they split.

Alba wanted a lipstick and found one in a geranium tone that looked wonderful on her angry adolescent pout. They headed back for the Martinez.

No sooner had they entered the hotel than five bouncers converged on them, recognized them, pirouetted and withdrew, the elegant choreography lasting no longer than a minute.

One of the assistant managers came toward them, smiling: "Very fashionable and, may I say, absolutely charming on Mademoiselle."

"Don't worry," Gorodish reassured him, "we'll change for dinner."

They went up to their room. "You going out heeled, tonight?" Alba asked worriedly.

"It isn't worth the risk. All we need is for some cop to stop us and we'd really be in trouble. Dress elegantly, you could carry a bazooka and nobody'd stop you, but wear leather and you're asking for trouble."

"Doesn't this remind you of the Vampires?"

"Yes, it does. Do you realize that if it hadn't been for them, we might never have met?"

"Oh, Serge, we'll love each other forever, won't we?"

CHAPTER

17

THEY ARRIVED SEPARATELY. MC5's "High Time" was screeching through the bar's hidden speakers as Alba came in. She perched on a barstool and looked around. Gorodish was already installed in one of the less vandalized booths. Alba sucked up a Coke, her expression nervous and withdrawn.

Out in the street rockers, motorcycles, choppers roared past and back again, chrome flaring white in the night. Inside the bar people took off, came back, went in and out.

Splendid Lola, Star of Stars, vision of purity and red-haired glamour, had not yet arrived.

As usual when working, Gorodish tried to empty his mind, tried to float along until the situation itself dictated his actions, hoping to be able to slip into the role he would have to play unburdened by any predefined attitudes.

Enter a space hero, an intergalactic Venus at his side. He with golden hair, golden glasses, glitter glued to his face, gleaming, glowing silver tights flowing into astronaut's boots of infinite blue. She ditto.

Gorodish watched two bouncers patrolling the clots of rockers and motorcycle gangs. The rules seemed simple enough: rockers on one side, cycle gangs on the other, and keep out of my face, Jack. It was a temporary truce, a fragile universe of social fragmentation and separation of the classes.

Rock heroes struck sparks in the dark: Queen, Hawkwind, Motorhead, Aerosmith: steel tempered by endless nights. And the incredible girls: Lola Black, Patti Smith, Deborah Harry, Nina Hagen, Pat Benatar, Kate Bush, Sappho.

At last she arrived, sat at the bar, downed a shot glass full of bourbon and let the music take her.

Suddenly Gorodish felt intimidated: this was a completely new sort of scam. Not daring to look at Alba, he rose and slid his leather-covered body between, through, around the other leather-covered bodies in the bar until he was standing next to Lola. He looked down at her.

For the last five minutes Alba had been messing around with a tall, snapped and zippered stud, a real catch, a beast but not impossible. She watched Lola climb down from the barstool and walk out with Gorodish: she had picked him up very, very fast. An idea flashed through Alba's mind, as quick and complex as a riff by Eddie Clarke. Gorodish disappeared through the red-lit doorway. Alba trembled with repressed rage and immediately went into action.

Gorodish walked down the street with Lola. She still seemed to be swinging to the sound of the music in the bar. He decided to play it like a slightly stupid rocker.

"We'll take my car," Lola said, in barely accented French.

"You got any grass?" Gorodish asked: a throwaway line.

"I'll roll us a joint later. There're too many cops around here."

"You American or English?"

"American."

Silence. They climbed into the Impala and Lola pulled away from the curb, the power steering squealing slightly. As they moved up the Croisette, Lola pushed a Sarah Vaughan tape into the car stereo.

"You like that?" she asked.

"Yes."

"You come here often?"

"No. I'm down here from Paris."

"You know the Zaza Club? It's a hard-rock dance club."

"No. How long's it been open?"

"I think it's new, but I've been there."

They were heading toward Antibes now.

"We'll park near the water; I really like it around there."

Gorodish watched Lola closely, a little disappointed that she seemed to lack the star quality, the presence, that he had expected. Perhaps one had to know her better. She didn't seem to want to talk: that made it easier.

As they neared the port Lola said, "You like Rimbaud?"

"Never heard of the dude," Gorodish replied.

"He's no dude, he's a writer, a poet. Don't you know *Le bateau ivre*? That's one of his poems."

"I'm more into music," Gorodish said, putting an end to the conversation.

A while later she said, "We'll go down to the rock beach. I love it down there."

"Whatever turns you on."

"Isn't Sarah's voice incredible?"

The car slowed and turned to the right. Lola parked in exactly the same spot she had the night before, pulled off one of her boots and took out a small hash pipe.

The moment had come. "Why did you dye your hair red, Lola?" Gorodish asked. "It was so much prettier black."

"Who's that: Lola?" she asked, unfazed.

"You don't think I picked you up by accident, do you?"

"I came with you because you don't really look like a rocker and I wanted to find out more about you," she said. "What're you after?"

"You mustn't give up, Lola. There are millions of people out there who love you, people who're waiting for you to sing again. I'm sure you really want to sing again."

"Okay, so you recognized me. I don't give a damn. All I wanted was a new life, and I've found it. So just forget the flattery, will you? Ever since my father put up that reward money there's all sorts of people been coming out of the woodwork. It's funny: everybody says they have my interests at heart, you know? You're like the rest: all you want is the money, right?"

"What about The Great Spirit of the Forest?"

"Yeah, well, he sort of runs things, tells me what to do. Did you ever meet him?"

"Not directly."

"And you don't know Rimbaud?"

For a long moment Gorodish said nothing, then: "I created every festival, every triumph, every play . . ."

"You *do* know Rimbaud. Do you always lie about everything?"

"Why are you running away?" Gorodish asked. "Weren't you happy on that island in the Seine?"

"Yes, but there wasn't any indoor plumbing."

"What about at your cabin in Big Sur?"

"That was different. You know a lot about me, don't you?"

"Two or three things . . ."

"You ought to listen to music more: that'd clear the shit out of your head."

"Look, Lola, I really wish you would trust me . . ."

"What do you want from me? Do you want me to go back to living the way I did before? I've given up all that crap. I've said everything I have to say, given everything I had to give. It's over now. I don't want it anymore. And there's no place for someone like you in my life either. I don't need anyone."

"Then what are we doing here?"

"I don't like making love in a bed."

Gorodish had dreamed a completely different sort of Lola. Suddenly he felt defeated, as if he'd wasted his time tracking down this person next to him. After all, he thought, trying to convince himself, some creative people use themselves up quickly. They give everything they have, they empty themselves of their very substance to produce a pure, shining, but limited, body of work.

Lola was watching him. She slid nearer and touched his arm. "Forget it," she said. "Just let yourself go. . . ."

Alba and the stud left the sounds of the Quickie Bar behind and walked toward the Croisette.

"What's your name?" he asked.

"Alba. What's yours?"

"Eddie." His face was scarred, an indication that he was the real thing. He moved closer to Alba and kissed her. She let him. He was a bit brutal and she found it rather unpleasant at first. Then, after a while, it got better.

"Wanna go for a ride?" He seemed sure of her answer.

"Okay."

Eddie led her to his brand-new Kawasaki 1000.

"Not too shabby," Alba said.

"Yeah. Only thing is: I'm still breaking her in. Can't push her past one ten, but she really moves."

"You have any money?"

"Enough for gas."

"You want me to go get some?"

"How much you got?"

"About five hundred francs, but it's at home."

Eddie climbed off the cycle. "Okay, babe: you got fifteen minutes."

He pulled out a Gauloise cigarette, tapped it gently on

the gas tank and watched Alba disappear down the street. Plans flashed through his head: five hundred francs would keep the night from being a total loss.

Alba ran toward the hotel, turning back every once in a while to make sure that Eddie was not following her.

She ran up to the room, crouched down next to the bed and slipped her hand between the springs. Her fingers touched the smooth, cold weight of the .45.

She checked to see that it was loaded and then, with some effort, managed to push the gun down into her right boot. Luckily, her jeans covered the bulge.

Alba counted the money in her pockets then hurried back to rejoin Eddie. Crossing the hotel lobby, she suddenly felt nervous, afraid that the .45 showed beneath her jeans.

Eddie was leaning against his treasure, his beauty, calmly smoking a cigarette. "That didn't take long," he said.

"It wasn't far," Alba answered, handing over the five hundred francs.

Eddie grabbed the money and slipped it into his jacket pocket. This pretty little thing was looking better by the minute.

"There's something I'd like to do," Alba said, her voice filled with sensual promise.

"What's that?" Eddie asked, the situation and the money making him feel especially generous.

"I have this ex-boyfriend who took off with this rich American girl who likes to get it on down by the rock beach at Antibes. How'd you like to take a run up there, see if we can find them? It'll be fun."

"Okay," Eddie said.

Alba climbed on behind him. He kicked the Kawasaki into life. The motor purred: nice kitty-cat.

Alba clutched Eddie's waist.

The air whistled past them. The lights of the city bypassed their retinas, reached directly into their brains and filled their heads with a continuous flash. Incredible. Alba's hair was a comet in the night. She imagined Gorodish, the Impala, the sea, Lola. Pain and humiliation rose from her gut and filled her body. They were probably doing it.

They would be making love . . .

The wind whipped the tears from her face.

CHAPTER

18

LOLA WAS BEAUTIFUL. SHE HELD Gorodish tightly and opened his shirt. He touched her breasts and kissed her.

Her lips were dead, passive. Gorodish felt a chill that almost paralyzed him. The Lola he had loved, that image of divinity, that woman made of fire and nerve ends, seemed to have disappeared, lost, somehow, in her flight, her withdrawal from the world.

"Don't you want me?" Lola asked with a small, throaty laugh.

Gorodish pulled away, looked directly into her eyes and said, "There's no real chemistry here. I think you'd better take me back."

"Whatever you say." Lola began to rebutton her blouse. Something hit Gorodish on the head. His vision blurred and he fell forward, landing between the steering wheel and Lola's lap.

"You took long enough," Lola said to Diamant.

"Not as long as you. I've been freezing my ass off out here for the last two hours."

"Where were you?"

"Over by the food stand. When you got here I hid behind those concrete blocks and listened to what he was saying. Some fascinating shit."

"Why didn't you hit him right away?"

"I told you, I wanted to find out what he knew."

"That million-dollar reward's really fucking us up. They're going to be after us like flies around a honey pot."

"I'm a good flyswatter," Diamant said. He opened the car door. "Come on. Help me put him in the trunk."

They dragged Gorodish from the front seat and hoisted him into the trunk. Diamant took the wheel, drove back to the coast road and headed for the main highway.

Eddie had hidden his cycle in the same spot where, earlier, Diamant had waited for the Chevy. Alba stood next to him, watching as Diamant moved out from behind the shadow of the cement blocks and toward the car.

"What'd they do to your ex?" Eddie asked.

"They're crazy."

"We're not going to let a couple of rich sonsabitches get away with that."

"Oh, Eddie, please, let's help him."

"Climb on," Eddie said, "we'll follow them."

Diamant was far too nervous to notice the motorcycle following him, its headlights off.

"Are you going to kill him?" Lola asked.

"Yeah, just like we did that old man in Paris. I'm not letting these leeches take any part of our action."

"What about the girl?"

"I'll take care of her later. First we have to find out exactly how much this guy knows. He may not be in it alone so we're going to have to make him talk."

"I'm getting scared. It was so smooth, everything was so slick, and now it's all falling apart. There's too many dead bodies behind us. The Great Spirit of the Forest is getting angry. He's going to punish us."

"Will you stop that shit?"

"I feel things you can't even begin to imagine."

Diamant lifted one hand from the wheel and slapped Lola's face. "Someday I'll get up on that stage," she cried, furious, "and there'll be a thousand, million guys after me, and I'll dump you!"

"*I'll* tell you when to get up on stage, baby. We're in this thing together until death do us part. I own you. So you just stay cool and let's leave The Great Spirit of the Forest out of it, okay?"

"Bastard."

They did not speak again until they reached the Moorish castle.

Even though Eddie was driving very carefully, Alba clung to him tightly.

"That their crib?" he asked.

"Yes."

"It's the fucking thousand and one nights," Eddie grinned. "This is going to be fun."

The Chevy pulled up to the front door. Eddie hid the cycle behind a stand of dwarf palms and they ran through the front gate, pushing their way through the heavy vegetation at the edge of the property, stopping occasionally to check what was happening in the Chevy. Lola and Diamant opened the trunk. Lola climbed up the front stairs, opened the main door, shut off the entry hall light, then came back to the car to help Diamant.

"Bastards," Eddie said. He took out a beautiful switchblade knife and opened it, muffling the click against the palm of his hand.

The blade gleamed.

"Eddie," Alba said, stopping him with a touch of her hand. "I've got something better than that."

Raising the leg of her jeans she pulled the .45 from her boot and placed its heavy metal weight in Eddie's hand.

"Shit! You're really something, babe! Beautiful! Where'd you get the iron?"

"Stole it from a house I visited last week."

Lola and Diamant dragged Gorodish up the stairs and into the Moorish palace. Lola closed the front door.

"Come on," Eddie said, taking Alba's hand, "let's take a look around. You know if they got a dog?"

"No, they don't."

"Good. Hey, they really must have some bucks. You *know* I'm not leaving here empty-handed."

"I'm glad you're with me," Alba said.

They made their way past a small grove of tall royal palms. Eddie examined the house with a practiced eye: several of the rooms were lit up.

"We'll get the drop on them, go in through the second-floor windows. There's a drainpipe: we oughta check and see if it'll hold us."

"It looks like they're going upstairs," Alba said.

A light had gone on in the large sitting room.

"Okay, we won't have to do it the hard way; we can go in through the garden. Maybe they forgot to lock the front door or something. You stay here; I'll be right back."

She did not hear him return. Eddie walked lightly, as if moving over a carpet of bubbles, his body bent forward as if he were searching for something he had lost. The .45 was clutched in his hand.

"What'd I tell you," he whispered. "The door's open. Let's go."

"Maybe we ought to wait awhile. My ex'll wake up soon and he'll be able to help us."

"Sure he will, if he's got a skull like an elephant."

"He's tough."

"What's he look like? Maybe I saw him. . . ."

"He's tall and sort of husky. He's wearing an old-fashioned aviator's helmet."

"Oh, yeah, he's there. That helmet probably protected his head when they clobbered him. Okay, we'll wait awhile. The 'Mericans aren't going anywhere. . . ."

CHAPTER

19

THEY SNEAKED INTO THE HOUSE, quietly closing the door behind them. Eddie crept forward, a cat stalking its prey, with Alba following behind.

An elaborate circular staircase, its steps covered with a worn blue runner, led to the second floor. They could hear muffled voices, the sound deadened by draperies, cushions, rugs.

Alba signaled to Eddie: she had heard something.

Gorodish was speaking:

". . . reach some sort of agreement . . ."

". . . all I want is the reward money . . ."

"It's my ex," Alba whispered. "Let's go."

"Stay behind me and watch where you put your feet," Eddie whispered back. "Here." He handed her the switchblade. "If they've got him tied up you cut him loose."

Alba was expecting Eddie to walk slowly, silently up the stairs. Instead, he ran up them two by two.

She followed, one step at a time.

The high arched door into the sitting room stood open. Eddie hesitated for a moment, fascinated by the luxury of the decor. He could see the Yank seated in a large armchair, sunk so far into the cushions that he seemed half his actual size. He was holding a gun on Alba's ex. The girl was standing behind a bar as elaborately carved as a mosque, mixing drinks.

Alba's ex lay sprawled on the carpet, about ten or twelve feet from the Yank's chair.

Eddie motioned Alba to stay where she was. Glancing down at the .45, he checked, for the tenth time, that the safety was off.

Then he sprang into the room.

"Don't move, man, or I'll waste you!" Eddie shouted.

The Yank plunged to the floor.

Three shots rang out: two from Eddie's gun, one from Diamant's.

A .45 does a lot of damage. One bullet crashed through a glass cabinet; its front window slid to the floor, intact. Another round hit Diamant in the throat, the impact catapulting him onto the coffee table which collapsed under his weight. He was dead.

Eddie slumped to his knees, holding the gun with one hand, his abdomen with the other.

Gorodish stood up.

Lola let go of the cocktail glass. It fell to the thick carpet and quietly smashed to pieces.

Eddie's hand slid toward the floor. His body folded forward.

Gorodish's head began to spin. He tried to steady himself on a side table and found himself back on the floor.

Gorodish watched as Lola walked toward Diamant, moving like a sleepwalker, her face pale and devoid of expression.

Eddie heard the music come UP, remembered a death scene he'd seen in some detective movie, a guy falling down church steps, he couldn't remember his name. Hell, he'd never had a very good memory.

Eddie looked down. His hand was covered with blood. "Bastard got me," he muttered. He saw Alba moving toward her ex.

The gun seemed to be floating high in the sky, a small black spot in that vast expanse of blue.

Hot damn, I'm dying in a mansion, Eddie thought, not bad. That chick he'd picked up tonight: awesome. He could've had her on that couch over there: it would've really been something. For a moment it looked as if there were three guns on the rug and then the world began to turn, began to look like that underground film he'd seen that one time, everything in double exposure.

The American bitch was probably going to try for the gun. He thought he saw it moving around, held in something light. Oh, yeah: her hand.

Weird, trying to lift your arm when you can't focus and all you can see are these colors sliding past, just before the black queen in her black cloak suddenly appeared.

His gun seemed to be pointing at the American chick, leading her, as if aiming at a moving target.

"No, Eddie, don't!" Alba shouted, running toward him.

Eddie thought he heard something just before he pulled the trigger. The shot was as loud as a cannon going off and the recoil tore the gun from his hand. But the space in front of his eyes was empty now: it was *clean;* no threat from that direction because the bitch was probably dead.

Eddie fell over on his side. The sky was filled with golden curlicues. He'd been in trouble ever since he could remember, but that stuff up there looked like paradise to him. There had to be worse bastards who'd made it; yeah, it was paradise, it was beautiful, and there was a blond angel bending over him, she was really built, and she said in this real sweet voice: "Eddie, Eddie . . ."

Priests were nuts: they'd always told him angels had no sex, but this one, no shit, he could see her tits under her T-shirt.

I did real good, dying like this, Eddie thought and reached for the angel's breasts.

Alba was holding Eddie in her arms. She felt a shudder run through him, then a jolt shake him, as if his body were letting go of the day's stress, letting sleep come.

"Serge, he's dead."

Gorodish managed to stand. He moved over to Lola.

"He, he," Alba said, "he shot her."

"A total fuckup," Gorodish said.

"Are you hurt?" Alba took refuge in Gorodish's arms and began to cry.

"All that work for nothing!" he said. "Damn! I had a bad feeling about this one from the very beginning." He held her tightly and patted her back. "Still, it could have been worse," he said. "Diamant would have killed me if you hadn't shown up with that boy."

"Poor Eddie."

"You followed me."

"Yes, well, sort of: he had a motorcycle."

"Someone may have heard the shots. We'd better get out of here."

"What about the police? They'll find fingerprints. . . ."

"I'll wipe off everything I touched, but we'll leave the rest just the way it is. There's nothing here to connect us with these people."

"What about Charon."

"He won't talk."

"I'm so sorry about Eddie. Poor guy, he'd just bought this really super motorcycle."

"Did anybody see you with him?"

"Nobody pays attention to anything at that bar, except the music. Let's get out of here: I can't stand it anymore."

She walked over to Lola's body. The dead girl's eyes were wide open and seemed to be staring up at Alba.

"We really messed up on this one," Alba said sadly.

"Let's go."

"How are we getting back to Cannes?"
"We'll walk. We can't take the Chevy or the motorcycle."
"Can you make it that far?"
"I'll manage. I'm glad you bought me that aviator's helmet."
Gorodish and Alba moved out of the sitting room toward the staircase. Suddenly, Gorodish froze. Someone was hammering on a door.

CHAPTER

20

THE FRONT DOOR'S NOT LOCKED," Alba said.

"It's coming from upstairs."

They ran up to the third floor and found themselves in a long, dim corridor faintly lit by small, Moorish lamps, its walls covered with etchings of harem scenes.

They came to a door with no key in the lock. Gorodish kicked it open. The door smashed against the inside wall.

A girl sat on the floor. She was trembling, leaning against a bed, her face white.

"I'm Lola Black," she said in a small, rasping voice.

Alba and Gorodish took in the black hair, the intensity of her expression, her hands, her fear. Alba helped Lola to her feet and held her tightly while waves of joy rose through her and tears of happiness filled her eyes.

Gorodish looked around the room, seeing the bars at the windows, the half-eaten apple, the ashtray filled with cigarette butts, the empty plate on a tray, the pile of ginger ale cans in one corner of the room. A photograph of Rimbaud was pinned to the wall.

Lola was wearing a dark dress with brightly colored panels in its godet skirt. "Who are you?" she asked, kissing Alba's brow.

"Friends," Gorodish answered.

"God," said Lola.

"We have to get out of here."

"All right."

Lola removed the photo of Rimbaud from the wall and held it tightly in her hand.

It was three in the morning and everything was quiet. Gorodish took a quick look around the grounds, then led them from the house.

"I used to be able to speak some French but I've forgotten most of it," Lola said. She was obviously upset.

"Can you walk?" Gorodish asked.

"I can run if I have to. Just get me out of here. Are they dead?"

"Yes."

Lola walked over to Gorodish and kissed him. "The whole thing's been really extraordinary, *tu sais.*"

Leaving the Moorish palace, they made their way to the main road, Gorodish leading them along the sidewalk that ran parallel to the railroad tracks.

"Is it far?" Lola asked.

"About a half hour's walk. If the police stop us, we'll say we decided to go for a stroll, all right? There shouldn't be any problem, but I don't want you to be scared."

"Okay," Lola said. "How'd you find me?"

"It's a long story," Gorodish answered.

"So's mine," Lola said, smiling bitterly.

"What do you want to do?" Alba asked.

"I don't know," Lola answered, "just breathe, I guess."

"We have to leave Cannes immediately," Gorodish said.

"We'll stop at the hotel, pick up our things and head north to our place in the country."

"It'll be good for her," Alba said. "She can rest for awhile, take it easy, take time to decide what she wants to do next."

Gorodish asked for the bill and they went upstairs to pack. Lola waited in the station wagon. She gazed out at the city, the lights, the sky, then lowered the car window and listened to the sea, as if hearing a new song for the first time. Suddenly feeling the need to see it with her own eyes, Lola got out of the station wagon, crossed the street and sat down on a balustrade overlooking the beach. The sand glowed, a secret light in the dark.

Alba's voice pierced the night like a moonbeam: "Come on, Lola, we're leaving!"

The streets were almost deserted. The three of them sat in the front seat as Gorodish drove toward the highway. "It's so good to be on the move again!" Lola said.

"We ought to change our clothes," Gorodish said. "We don't want to be stopped by the cops."

They parked and Alba and Gorodish changed into less inflammatory clothing. A few minutes later they were on the road again.

"How did you find me?" Lola asked.

"I have a news bureau," Gorodish explained. "A man who used to go fishing near Poissy tried to sell me some information; he claimed that you were alive. Alba and I went to see a movie about you and decided to look into it. Then our informant was murdered. By Diamant."

"That's the worst son of a bitch you'd ever hope to meet," Lola said.

"We found Ile aux Dames and the house you'd been living in, and we met the old man who rents out boats."

"That's Diamant's father."

"Really?" Alba exclaimed.

"Didn't you know?"

"No. All we knew was that he was working with Diamant," Gorodish said. "We met him after our informant was killed, and you'd already gone. We managed to find your address and followed Diamant when he came to the post office to pick up a package the old man sent you. But he spotted us and set a trap for me. Without Alba's help he would have killed me, too."

"Why did you get involved in this in the first place?" Lola asked. "Why did you risk your lives?"

"For the money," Gorodish said, determined to tell the truth this once.

"What money?"

"Your father's put up a million-dollar reward for whoever finds you."

"Incredible. I'm glad you came when you did; Diamant would have wound up killing me, too."

Alba was listening quietly, her arms around Lola's neck.

"It's so strange, I never thought people like you, people who own a news bureau and all, would take that kind of chance, even for that amount of money. How do you say it in French: *flouze*?"

"*Flouze*," Alba said approvingly.

"My own story's much longer and more complicated, and just awful. I can't seem to get it straight in my head yet. Maybe if I told it from the beginning it would help. I'd played this concert at Family Dog in San Francisco and afterward I had a breakdown, *tu sais,* so I decided to take some time off at my cabin in Big Sur, and I *annullé*-ed the tour.

"I needed some time to meditate in the woods; it's really gorgeous there, and I was living alone. One night this guy, Diamant, showed up. He had a gun and said he was taking me away. He gave me something to drink; it must have had a pile of downers in it; anyway, I went on the nod and he put me in his car and drove down to Los Angeles where he had a chartered plane waiting.

"We flew down to Mexico, then he drove us to a small port on the Gulf Coast and we got on a sailboat. I think it took us about two weeks to cross the Atlantic, I'm not too clear on that part of it. There were these other two men on the boat, sailors, I think. Anyway, we reached this port somewhere in the north of France and he drove me to his father's island and we settled down in that shack.

"I didn't understand what was going on. There was this other girl on the island. She was American, too, and he called her Lola. She was from Chicago and looked just like me. What do they call that: a double? It was weird, the two of us together in that house.

"After I'd been there a few days, Diamant told me he'd met the girl in Chicago, picked her up on the street. He was dealing heroin then; he'd been in the States for a few years, and he liked my music, so when he met the girl he thought she was me. She told him she wasn't Lola Black; she was working as a salesgirl at Saks Fifth Avenue, but he got friendly with her and decided to use her. He knew I liked Rimbaud and like that, so he worked out this plan to kidnap me.

"He wanted this other girl to take my place; he was planning to put her onstage and pocket all the concert fees, but she had to learn to do everything the way I did, and I was supposed to teach her how to sing. We worked at it every day but she didn't have much of a voice. We used my old tapes, he'd brought in a tape recorder, and I tried to teach her all my songs. I was also supposed to tell her everything about me, starting way back in my childhood. She tried to learn how to walk like me and talk like me and move like me. Diamant thought she was almost ready and made me help him write a letter to the *Washington Post.* He knew my father's rich and he wanted to get his hands on that money, too.

"He was planning to take the girl back to the States. She would have taken my place and he would have had my father's money, and the inheritance, and the royalties from the records, and the concert fees. He knew it would take awhile to get things organized and working smoothly, but when they were, the old man would have killed me, and that would have been that."

"It's not a bad plan," Gorodish said.

"He wasn't stupid. But she was kind of dumb."

"It must have been terrible for you," Alba said.

"He was a horror. He used to beat me, and wouldn't give me anything to eat if I didn't do what he said. When I followed orders, he'd let me have whatever I wanted, but I couldn't escape and the old man watched me whenever Diamant went away for a few days."

"What about the girl?"

"She was kind of nice to me, but she was afraid of him. He'd beat her up whenever she forgot to walk like me, but she was in love with him, too, so that made it more complicated."

"Are you going to sing again?" Alba asked.

"Oh, I've been going crazy, not being able to sing. But I've had plenty of time to write some new songs these last six months. I've got eleven of them up here in my head; I think they're the best things I've ever done."

"Serge is a musician."

"I play the piano," Gorodish smiled. "Haydn, Beethoven, Schumann. . . ."

"I love classical music. I had a boyfriend who played cello with the Chicago Symphony Orchestra. Do you have a piano at your place?"

"Yes."

"Good. I'll be able to write out the new songs."

"How did you ever manage to get through the days?"

"Oh, there's always some way to make the time pass, even if you're in prison. You live in your head a lot, though it's really painful. How are you going to get the money from my father?"

"I don't know," Gorodish said. "Do you have any suggestions?"

"You could call him and let me talk to him. Then you could tell him to come to Paris with the money, but to keep quiet about it and not let anybody know."

"That's fairly straightforward," Gorodish said, "but we must make sure nobody knows that you've been found, nor where, nor when."

"We can pretend you found me somewhere else, in another country. Or we could go back to the States before we call my father."

"I think that might be too dangerous, but let me think it over."

"We could even make it a round trip. I'd like to stay with you awhile. I really like France, you know. In fact, I think I'll do my first concert here, at the Paris Pavilion. I'll bring the band over. Oh, that's a good idea! You know, with all the rehearsing I've been doing, I could go onstage right now if I had to."

Gorodish tried to think of some other way to arrange the exchange. He was wary of the French police: perhaps it would be more prudent for them to go to the United States. He would have to pick up the money as far from Cannes as possible: there could be no link between Lola's reappearance and what the police would undoubtedly call a triple murder. He was certain they would not notice the resemblance between Lola's double and the singer, and if Diamant had a record in France, the police would treat it as a drug-related killing.

They reached Lyon a little after dawn. Lola was hungry so they stopped for breakfast: a bottle of Burgundy and *rosette* tripe sausage for Lola, ham for Gorodish, and six croissants and hot chocolate for Alba.

Several cups of coffee later, they were on the road again.

• • •

Gorodish and Alba were fascinated by Lola and could not stop staring at her. An atmosphere of complicity and affection began to grow among the three of them.

When they neared Beaune, Lola asked Gorodish to leave the highway and drive through the town.

Later, the long winding road made Lola and Alba sleepy. They climbed into the backseat and fell asleep in each other's arms. From time to time, Gorodish glanced at them in the rearview mirror. Then, turning his eyes to the road again, he tried to figure out a way to approach Monsieur Nash.

It was three in the afternoon when they turned off the highway at Fontainebleau. The country house was not far.

CHAPTER

21

GORODISH WOKE AT EIGHT IN the morning, drank two large mugs of coffee then telephoned and left a message for the man who would help launder the reward money. Monsieur Blaise was a genius at moving millions of francs from France to Swiss bank accounts without leaving the slightest trace of their passage.

Monsieur Blaise returned Gorodish's call promptly, telephoning from a public booth: "Yes, sir, and how much will it be this time?"

"One million dollars, coming in from the United States."

"From which city?"

"Detroit."

"Ah, very good. I have a contact there who will be able to expedite matters. I should be able to handle the entire transaction myself."

"I'd prefer to take delivery of the merchandise here in France, before you become involved."

"I understand your anxiety, but the situation is a bit awkward at the moment. May I suggest an alternative solution to your problem?"

"Please do."

"You might consider moving the consignment through my conduit in Barcelona. Your American contact should have absolutely no problem bringing it into Spain from the United States."

"Excellent. I'll start things moving at my end. Please telephone me again tonight, at the country house."

Gorodish made breakfast, then went upstairs to wake Lola and his nymph.

It was raining, but the furnace had run all night and the house was warm.

A night's rest had transformed Lola. Her face was relaxed now and her body seemed to radiate power. She devoured the breakfast, smoked a dozen Gauloise cigarettes and then sang a few of her new songs for Alba and Gorodish.

"Oh, Serge, I can't wait for the Paris concert! I bet I could get ready in three weeks, if my musicians aren't tied up with other gigs . . ."

"The sooner the better," Gorodish agreed. "There are only two things left to arrange: first, it would be a lot safer for all of us if you surfaced somewhere else other than France. Don't forget: we've left three bodies behind us. We must let the story break elsewhere; that way it will look as if you decided to come here after you reappeared. I've been thinking it over and it seems to me that you better show up in the United States. The second thing is: I want that million dollars before you leave here."

"Whatever you say," Lola agreed. "I'm still getting the better part of this deal."

"Let's call your father now. I've decided to make the switch in Spain. You can fly from there to Mexico, or directly to the States, if you want."

"I don't have my passport. Diamant tore it up."

"That's no problem," Gorodish said. "We'd have had to

give you a new passport anyway, just to make sure nobody could trace you."

"Serge, you're too much."

"I'll take care of the passport," Gorodish said. "Let's call your father now. You talk to him first, then I'll take it from there."

Gorodish waited patiently until the cries and squeals of reunion were over. Then he spoke with Monsieur Nash.

"Meet me in Barcelona three days from today, noon, at the Picasso Museum."

"Okay."

"Can you transfer the money to a Spanish bank and give it to me in cash?"

"Sure."

"Check into the Hotel Colón. It'll be easier for me to get in touch with you there."

"Fine."

"Your father isn't very talkative," Gorodish said.

"I know. He used to talk a bit more when I was living at home, but since I moved out . . . But he's very successful in his business."

They spent the night in a hotel near the Spanish border, starting off again at dawn in order to be on time for the meeting in Barcelona. They crossed the border, the first test of Lola's new passport, with no problem. When day broke they were happily surprised to see a clear, blue sky. It was hot.

They entered Barcelona by the port road. Two tall towers, linked by an aerial tram, dominated the skyline. Gorodish had ridden the tram several years earlier: he remembered the extraordinary view it afforded of docked ships and the sea.

They sat at a sidewalk café at the edge of a beautiful plaza. A fountain and several palm trees stood at its center.

"We ought to travel more often," said Alba, taking in the strange new sights.

"We could stay here for a few days while we wait for Lola to return," Gorodish offered.

"I'd like to stay at your house when I come back for the concert," Lola said.

"Let's see how things go," Gorodish replied. "We have to be very careful."

He read through the newspaper he had bought before crossing the French border. There were several articles about "the mysterious murders in Cannes." He took some comfort in the fact that the police had identified Diamant as a drug dealer and had learned the American girl's real name. Nobody seemed to have noticed her resemblance to Lola and all the stories played up the drug-war angle.

Gorodish left Lola and Alba for a half hour, returning with Lola's airplane ticket for Mexico. She would cross the border at Tijuana and go back to Big Sur before announcing her return. They agreed that she would explain her disappearance by continuous, confusing references to communing with The Great Spirit of the Forest.

At a quarter to twelve Gorodish, Alba and Lola walked into the Picasso Museum. While they waited they examined the artist's early works, mostly landscapes painted on small wood panels and the bottom of cigar boxes.

At noon, a taxi drew up in front of the museum and a tall, red-faced man with a tuft of bluish-gray hair got out. His mouth was so large, his smile so white and overpowering, that it looked as if it had been carved from an elephant's tusk. Gorodish felt as if he were staring at, minimum, sixty teeth.

Lola threw herself into her father's arms. He held her tightly and said: "Virginia, my darling. . . ."

Lola was weeping. Gorodish waited until she calmed down before walking over to Monsieur Nash. The American shook Gorodish's hand for a good thirty seconds, all the while displaying that double row of fangs. Gorodish had to admit it: the man had personality.

"Everything's been arranged," Monsieur Nash said in highly accented French. "If it's all right with you, we'll meet at this address"—he held out a card—"with your representative, and mine."

"When?"

"Whenever you like."

"Six o'clock?"

"Okay. I'd like to ask a favor: I want to spend the rest of the day with Virginia."

"No," Gorodish said firmly.

"Okay," Nash said. "Business is business. Do they say that where you come from?"

"Absolutely."

"Good," said Nash, kissing his daughter and heading back to the waiting taxi without a backward glance.

"You were so harsh, Serge," Alba said, embarrassed.

"It's okay with me," Lola said. "I love my father but we don't really have very much to say to each other. After one hour together we either wind up going to a movie or we start to fight. It's better this way. I'll see him tonight, or tomorrow, before I get on the plane."

"I know a good restaurant near the port," Gorodish said. "Let's have lunch."

They ordered enormous paellas and large carafes of wine. Gorodish asked Lola to tell them the story of her life. She was an only child; her mother was dead.

That afternoon they took the aerial tram and saw the cargo ships in the harbor.

Alba insisted they visit the reproduction of Christopher Columbus's galleon.

Gorodish seemed strangely withdrawn. Ideas were racing through his head.

CHAPTER

22

THE TRANSFER OF FUNDS FROM Daddy Nash to Gorodish was a simple transaction. It took only a few hours for the one million dollars to be tucked safely away in Gorodish's Swiss bank account. After which, Lola boarded the plane for Mexico.

Three days later articles began appearing in the papers reporting that a guru in Big Sur claimed to have seen the ghost of Lola Black wandering along the beach. Immediately after, the news came clattering across teletypes all over the world:

GREAT SPIRIT OF FOREST FREES LOLA BLACK

Gorodish and Alba listened to the news breaks and special reports and read every paper on the newsstands.

Lola played her part beautifully: she stonewalled, covering up the truth of her disappearance with a thick layer of mysterio-mytho-Amer-Indian delirium. The reporters were reduced to quoting her.

Then came news that Guzzy Smith, Lola and her band were together again, rehearsing eleven new songs that the Star of Stars had written for her comeback performance in France. Local radio stations began playing cuts from old Lola Black albums and running announcements publicizing the upcoming concert at the Paris Pavilion.

Hounded by the press, Daddy Nash released a statement saying that his daughter's reappearance was her own doing, and denying that he had paid one red cent in ransom.

Lines of desperate cops were completely overwhelmed as they tried to control the three hundred thousand fans who had come to Roissy Airport, outside Paris.

Gorodish and Alba, riding in the long black limousine Lola had demanded the concert's sponsors provide, drove slowly through the crowd. It took them a good fifteen minutes to reach the official parking area where three other limos stood waiting. The French secret service couldn't have organized it better.

Since they had nothing to do before the chartered plane arrived, the longhairs, the shaved heads, the rockers and the punks gave Alba a standing ovation as she slithered out of the limo, dressed to kill in mega-fifties style. A veil hid her blond nymph's face from the public's eyes.

"Who's that?"

"Gotta be some star."

"Isn't that whatshername?"

Gorodish thought it more prudent to wait in the car.

Heavy metal gates led into the customs area. Flashbulbs. Doors slid open. In an attempt to calm the fans, Alba was hustled out of sight and into an empty office.

The crowd fell silent.

Sitting Bull Plastic was the first to appear, his face almost hidden under a war bonnet, his guitar slung from a strap over his shoulder. The crowd began to scream.

A few seconds later Tommy Bonaparte appeared, his bishop's miter tilted to the left, a Swiss cuckoo clock in his hands. The crowd immediately dug that this was the latest, hottest addition to his array of percussion instruments. Reporters scribbled notes. An in-depth analysis of this new development would fill the pages of rock magazines around the world.

The screaming grew louder.

Preceded by an interracial assortment of groupies, Mexico Flat came down the ramp. He had shaved his greasy black do and changed his bridal gown for a newer model: more grist for the critics' mill.

Several hundred camera lenses focused on the doorway through which the high priestess of rock would soon appear.

The crowd exploded. There she was: Lola. Dressed in leather, dark goddess of rock, sublime and fragile, her golden lips smiling. Flashbulbs. She lifted her arms toward the sky and walked past the paralyzed customs officials, entering the main lobby of the terminal with a savage cry of greeting bursting from her throat:

"Hi!"

Her musicians surrounded her. Photographers broke through the barriers. Microphones pointed in her direction. Lola moved down a corridor of human bodies straining toward her. Despite the best efforts of the police, the edges of the corridor were beginning to give. Sheer delirium.

Spellbound by Lola's appearance, Alba remained hidden in the office, hesitating to detract from the rock diva's entrance. Then, suddenly, she couldn't stand it anymore. Alba ran toward her friend, calling her name. Lola heard her above the crowd noise and turned.

They embraced. The photographers captured the intensity of the greeting. "Whoozat?" they asked.

A bouquet of roses appeared from somewhere within the

crowd. Lola accepted it, blowing kisses. A rent-a-cop urged her forward, toward the limousine, motioning to her to hurry as the corridor through the crowd began to narrow.

The entourage began to run just as Daddy Nash appeared in the doorway of the plane. He trotted to catch up.

The band's monster sound system and instruments were unloaded from the chartered plane and placed on a truck.

Sitting Bull Plastic and Tommy Bonaparte removed their headgear and clambered into the first limousine, accompanied by their groupies. Guzzy Smith and Mexico Flat rode in the second car. Daddy Nash rode alone in the third.

Lola kissed Gorodish and Alba.

The line of cars began to move. Fans raced toward them, seemingly determined to throw themselves beneath the wheels.

Lola waved. The limos reached the highway and quickly drove toward an unknown destination.

An hour later the four cars drove up the driveway leading to Gorodish's country house.

He had bought extra beds, bribed that season's chicest, most hotly disputed African chef and hired two maids.

The only thing he hadn't counted on was the presence of Lola's father.

Alba immediately set about making friends with the musicians.

Gorodish was a little nervous about his piano, but so far nobody had laid a hand on it.

They sat on the couches in front of the fireplace. "We're really going to be able to get some work done out here," Lola said.

Visibly angry, Daddy Nash went up to his room and didn't come out again until dinner was served.

"Why did he come with you?" Gorodish asked.

"I don't know," Lola said. "Daddy told me he wanted to see a concert. He can't stand the band, but he's been hanging around us for the last three days. I'm getting fed up, know what I mean? Although, I have to admit he handled all those TV interviews real well. Oh, I'm so glad to see you again!" Lola kissed Alba.

Sitting Bull Plastic groped one of the groupies as she rolled a joint large enough to turn on the French army. A sweet odor filled the air. Gorodish uncorked several bottles of champagne.

"Play us a sonata," Lola urged. The musicians uttered guttural cries, a standard sign of their curiosity and approval.

Feeling no pain, Gorodish rose, sat down at the piano and began to pick through his music. He finally found a tune that pleased him and began to play. It was the First Beethoven Piano Sonata.

After the first few measures, Tommy Bonaparte began to drum on the couch, on the hassock, on the floor, on anything within reach of his hands. Despite frantic signals from Alba the drumming grew louder.

Gorodish finished the first movement.

"Not bad," said Mexico Flat, "but it could use a bass line behind it."

Gorodish burst out laughing and picked up his glass of champagne.

Sitting Bull Plastic suddenly abandoned his groupie and joined Alba on the other couch. "I like French girls," he said, in guise of foreplay. "Wanna sleep with me tonight?"

"Sure. When you learn to play a Beethoven sonata," Alba said, smiling.

Sitting Bull stuck out his tongue and went back to his red-haired groupie.

Food appeared on the table. Gorodish had bought fifty different kinds of cheese and several dozen bottles of fine wine. Lola began sampling the wine and picking at the cheese. When they finally sat down to eat she had already downed an entire Camembert and a small Brie.

"Alba, would you please get my father?" Lola asked.

In answer to her knock, Daddy Nash tore open his bedroom door.

"Won't you come to the table, Monsieur Nash?" Alba asked with her best stewardess smile.

"They're all shit," the old man said, but finally condescended to come to dinner.

Gorodish tried to calm him, to no avail. A groupie brought him a glass of champagne liberally spiked with a hit of LSD purchased from a perfectly respectable Swiss pharmaceutical house.

"I know a really nice man," Alba said; "his name's Phil Mann. Could I call and ask him over? You know him, don't you, Lola?"

"Yes. I spent the night with him a long time ago. What's he been doing?"

"He writes articles for rock magazines and has this really great television show."

"He's good," Guzzy said, speaking for the first time. "Tell him to come over. He'll get an exclu. Better yet, give me his number and *I'll* ask him over."

Ecstatic at having been invited to the party, Phil Mann arrived just in time for dessert, his cameraman and sound man in tow. They hurriedly nibbled a little something, then, as soon as the instruments were tuned and the musicians ready, rolled tape.

Lola sang three new songs, her energy making the walls shake.

Daddy Nash had his nose buried in a piece of Roquefort, fascinated by the sight of mold moving through the crevices. He burst out laughing, a harsh laugh that was covered by the thundering chords of a new song called "Alba."

Daddy Nash picked up a long kitchen knife and began hacking at the cheese. Growing more frantic, he beheaded a champagne glass. He cackled, then stopped and thought for a long moment, a moment that seemed to stretch before him into infinity.

Daddy Nash began talking to himself, asking and answering questions in two different voices.

He stabbed the table.

Lost in the music, Gorodish and Alba paid no attention to him, but when the music stopped, an electrifying scream filled the room. Everybody froze.

Daddy Nash headed toward Lola, the knife in his hand hacking at invisible objects standing between him and his daughter. He swore, and Lola backed into a corner. The blade seemed to be cutting the space before her into smaller and smaller pieces.

She managed to dodge the first slash.

Gorodish aimed a *savate* kick at Daddy Nash. Daddy Nash merely shook his head and turned to confront Gorodish.

Gorodish kicked him in the belly. Daddy Nash dropped to the floor. The red-haired groupie began to wail: "It's my fault! I slipped him some acid!"

Everyone looked at her, then away again: she had ceased to exist.

Gorodish took the knife from Daddy Nash's hand. The man lay on the floor, passive, his face as placid as a baby's.

Lola's face was ashen.

Gorodish lifted the industrialist. "Come with me, Alba," he said.

They carried Nash back up to his room and placed him on the bed. Alba pressed a cool compress to his forehead. The millionaire was delirious now, muttering disjointed words. Little by little, Gorodish began to discern a pattern to his mumbling.

"Go get your tape recorder and bring it here," he said. Alba came back with the tape recorder and turned it on.

"Go downstairs and take care of our guests," Gorodish said. "I want to be alone with Monsieur Nash."

Alba closed the door behind her.

Daddy Nash seemed terrified of the overhead light. Gorodish turned on the bedside lamp, plunging the rest of the room into shadow and darkness. He tried to reassure the man, saying, "Go with it, don't fight it, let the images come, talk, you can handle it, talk, you'll feel better. . . ."

"You dumb prick, you don't understand anything. She's always been a whore, from the day she was born . . . you know who I'm talking about . . . that cunt, Virginia, Virginia Nash . . . even before she was Lola Black . . . rotten, rotten to the bone. . . . I was crazy about my wife, you understand, don't you? . . . My wife was beautiful . . . I have her picture here, somewhere . . . her name was Daisy . . . delicate, smart, that whore killed her . . . she wasn't even thirty-one years old! . . . I'd married her the year before and that whore killed her . . . in childbirth. . . . Daisy died in the delivery room and left me with the baby . . . but she didn't die, no, she kept on growing and I wanted her dead because she was evil. . . . I tried to drown her but she could swim. . . . I tried buying her a sports car when she turned sixteen. . . . I tried everything but she was too rotten to die. . . . She was good in school, good at university. . . . I had the money, I sent her to Harvard Business School; I thought she was so evil she'd probably do well in business, take my place one day, run the Nash empire. I even began to think maybe she deserved to live . . . stupid, stupid. Don't you think I was stupid? It fell apart; she started playing that music at the university and all those others, rotten, evil . . . they came to her and stayed with her. She made a porno film; it played in Detroit and everyone saw it. She took drugs. She did time in prison. Her name in the papers and then she became famous and all the evil, all the rottenness, all the vice smearing Detroit and America. She sang at protest marches against the Vietnam War, she did everything. . . . I kept hoping she'd take an overdose and die, but nothing could kill her and I was going crazy, everybody watching her, so I paid a man to kill her,

I gave him a lot of money. His name was Diamant, he was a Frenchman, too, and he was rotten because he didn't do it. They found her body in the ocean and I was finally at peace, but I couldn't be sure it was Virginia and then I saw the letter in the *Washington Post* and I knew she was still alive and I had a heart attack. I offered a million dollars to find her and you found her and I wanted her found because I'd decided to kill her myself, wait for the right moment and kill her. There, on that chair, in my kit, there's enough poison to kill everybody, like the Jim Jones cult in Guyana, I thought everyone would die, but the devil saved her again and I couldn't kill her. You understand, don't you?"

Nash began to sob.

Gorodish rose, opened the leather toilet kit and found the bottle of poison. Then he turned off the tape recorder and said:

"We'll talk about this tomorrow."

Pressed tightly against each other, Gorodish and Alba lay in the wide bed. The house was quiet; sunrise was near.

"How're we doing financially?" Alba asked after a particularly long and liquid kiss.

"You're such a romantic."

"Well, we do have to think about the future, don't we?"

"I know you: you're up to something."

Alba nibbled at Gorodish's nose, then began to whisper, her tongue flicking at his ear, a sweet comma punctuating her words.

"It seems to me that the Americans have a better grasp of financial matters than we do. Did you notice how Daddy Nash handed over all that cash? It was as if he were tossing a tip to a doorman. I bet there are hundreds more like him over there. And it's where Horowitz and Serkin live: I'm sure you'd like it. And there's all that space. . . . I've been feeling so hemmed in lately, and frustrated with all that old money tucked away where we can't get our hands on it. . . ."

"You may have a point, but would you please stop tickling my ear?"

"We'll buy a Cadillac convertible and a Steinway turbo and you'll finally show me how to do it . . . you promised, for my fourteenth birthday . . . and we'll have a place at the beach and fifty credit cards and hundreds of books."

"Books?"

"I've been feeling that I need to shut myself away for a while and just read and read and read. . . ."

"All right," Gorodish said, "we'll leave the day after the concert. What'll it be: New York or Los Angeles?"

"Let's start with Los Angeles," said Alba.

About the Author

WHO IS "DELACORTA"? THAT WAS THE QUESTION THAT OCCUPIED Parisian literary circles upon the publication of *Diva* in France. After a year of speculation and mystery, the truth came out: Delacorta is the pen name of Daniel Odier, a young Swiss novelist and screenwriter about whom Anaïs Nin once wrote, "He is an outstanding writer and a dazzling poet."

Born in Geneva in 1945, Daniel Odier studied painting in Rome, received his university degree in Paris and worked as a music critic for a leading Swiss newspaper before taking off for a tour of Asia which resulted in a book on Taoism. His first book, *The Job: Interviews with William Burroughs,* was published in the United States in 1969. Since then he has published seven novels in France under his real name, two of which have become the basis for motion pictures by director Alain Tanner, and *Broken Dreams,* which will be made by director John Boorman. As Delacorta, he has written four books, *Diva, Nana, Luna* and *Lola;* the last has been made into a movie by French national television. He is now at work on the fifth installment of the escapades of Alba and Gorodish.

Mr. Odier teaches comparative literature at the University of Tulsa in Oklahoma, where he resides with his wife, the violinist Nell Gotkovsky.